PEOPLE OF GOD
FOR ALL OF GOD'S PEOPLE:
Witnessing to Unity at the Service of Justice

PEOPLE OF GOD
FOR ALL OF GOD'S PEOPLE:

Witnessing to Unity at the Service of Justice

Editors

Alwan Masih

Sudipta Singh

Compilation of Papers presented during
Mission Conference–2010
on the occasion of 40 years celebrations of
The Church of North India

THE CHURCH OF NORTH INDIA SYNOD
2011

People of God for All of God's People: Witnessing to Unity at the Service of Justice – published by the Rev. Dr. Ashish Amos of the Indian Society for Promoting Christian Knowledge (ISPCK), Post Box 1585, 1654, Madarsa Road, Kashmere Gate, Delhi-110006, for The Church of North India Synod, CNI Bhavan, 16 Pandit Pant Marg, Delhi-110001.

ISBN: 978-81-8465-183-6

Laser typeset at **ISPCK,** Post Box 1585, 1654, Madarsa Road, Kashmere Gate, Delhi-110006.
Tel: 23866323, Fax: 91-11-23865490
e-mail: ashish@ispck.org.in • ella@ispck.org.in
website: www.ispck.org.in

Contents

Foreword

The church exists because of God's mission, not ours. It is God who has called the church into being. It is through the church, the people of God, that God intends to carry out the Divine plan for the redemption of the world. Therefore, the mission of the church is to discern and to participate in God's mission. It needs to be rooted in Jesus Christ, grounded in his incarnate being and mission in order that it may be determined in its inner and outer life through participation in the life and ministry of Jesus Christ. The church, as the community of men and women filled with the presence of the Spirit, partaking of the fullness of the blessings and riches of God, has been sent out in the power of the Spirit to live out the divine life and love among humankind and creation as the bodily instrument and image of Christ in the world and the one comprehensive communion of the Spirit. In short, the church exists in Christ for mission to the world. It is not, merely that the church has a mission, but that the church exists for mission - ecclesiology and missiology, in Christ, are inseparably linked and grounded in the person and work of Jesus.

In this mission, the church is both like and unlike the ministry of the historical Jesus. It is rooted in it and patterned after it, and in a real sense shares in it. But it is a ministry of the redeemed, whereas the ministry of Jesus is that of the redeemer. As the company of Jesus' disciples in the world, the church is sent in the Holy Spirit to the world, participating in the ministry that Jesus is now doing there to fulfill God's mission to call all people from union to communion with God. The church does this work by both being and proclaiming the good news to the world. We see this purpose unfolding in Jesus' sending of his first disciples. According to Torrance, "the disciples were permitted to baptize, to go forth as Jesus' representatives bearing the proclamation of the kingdom on their lips and with authority to heal and forgive sins in his name". Indeed, the church, Jesus, and Jesus' mission are inseparably linked: The being and nature of the church are equally inseparable from its mission, that is, its sending by Christ on the mission of the love of God, just as the sending of Christ by the Father is inseparable from his being and nature as the incarnate Son. Through the work of Jesus, in the Spirit, within the church, the church becomes itself a communion of love through which the life of God flows out in love toward every human being. As he is, so are we in this world. As we celebrate forty years of our existence as a united and uniting church, we must come together to reflect whether our mission engagement has been in line with these thoughts and thereby plan our missional engagement for the years to come.

I record my pleasure of being part of such a historic mission conference which helped us, as individuals and also as a church, to look back, realize, strategize and envision a vision beyond forty. I am hopeful that those who could not be part of this gathering can get the inputs shared by God's people engaged in the prophetic mission of God published in this report.

Shalom in Christ!

The Most Rev. Dr. Purely Lyngdoh
Moderator
Church of North India

Preface

When we talk about mission or missions we tend to think of the church as being a sending agency or support agency for missionaries. In fact, mission, and with it the church, is God's very own work. We cannot speak of the 'mission of the church,' even less of 'our mission.' Both the church and the mission have their source in the loving will of God. Therefore we can speak of church and mission always only with the understanding that they are not independent entities. Both are only tools of God, instruments through which God carries out His mission. The church must first in obedience fulfill God's missionary intention. Only then can she speak of her mission, since her mission is then included in the Missio Dei.

The mission in which we are called as God's people to participate is work that belongs to God, it is God's mission (*Missio Dei*). So, if God is the initiator of the mission, and God calls and sends the church to participate in this mission – then the church exists for God and God's purposes. The Church has no purpose or mission of its own, unless it submits itself to the redemptive mission of the Living God. It is a biblical understanding we need to rediscover if we are to be the people of God in the world, otherwise we are merely a people who have an association with God – but not the people of God.

If it is true that God intends the mission since he carries out the mission, then the church can be God's vessel and tool only if she surrenders herself to His purpose. If she disassociates herself from this concern of God, she becomes disobedient and can no longer be church in the divine sense. There is no participation in Christ without participation in God's mission to the world. Hence the church is not called on to decide whether she will carry on the mission or not. She can only decide for herself whether she wants to be church. She should not determine by her own when, where, and how missions will be carried out, for the mission is divinely guided, as is shown in Acts. Thus mission is based on the activity that God initiates and completes. It means that mission is not merely one activity amongst others that we engage in as the people of God. Rather, mission is the core understanding of who we are as the people of God in the world – God has called us out of the world, set us apart as the people of God, filled us with the Holy Spirit, to be the unique community of recreated humanity through Jesus Christ. As this community that has its identity centered in Christ, we are called not to participate in ministries of our own choosing, but to participate with God in whatever and wherever God sends us for the accomplishing of God's redemptive purpose of reconciling humanity to himself and making all things new. This mission of God's is all focused and accomplished in and through Jesus Christ.

We, as the body of Christ, exist for God alone and for what God seeks to accomplish in recreating humanity and all creation. The needs of the world do not set the agenda for our ministry, rather it is in our serving of God that we participate in what impassions the heart of God – it is because God loves the world that not only did he send the Son, God also continues to send the people.

These are some of the affirmations that can be summarized from the Mission Conference held at Hislop College, Nagpur on 12th and 13th of October 2010 in celebration of our forty years of United Journey as a Church since its union on 29th November 1970. Therefore, we take it as a duty and responsibility to be thankful to God for His guidance and provision of resource people so that we could have a meaningful conference. Our thanks are due to Rev. Dr. Roger Gaikwad, Rev. Dr. habil James Massey, Rev. Dn. Philip Vinod Peacock, Rt. Rev. S. R. Cutting, Ms. Sadhona Ganguli, Mr. Philip Jadhav, Rev. Dr. Richard Fee, Rev. Dr. Vinita Eusebius, Rev. Dr. Daniel Premkumar and Dr. Shailendra Awale for their insightful presentations that helped the delegates to re-envision the mission of the church beyond forty. We are also grateful to our colleagues in the Programme Office for their hard work in editing the texts submitted by the presenters so that a proper volume could be produced of the report. We are sure that the inputs shared in this volume by the resource people will challenge us to be "People of God for All of God's People: Witnessing to Unity at the service of justice" which was the theme of the Conference.

Peace in Christ!

Mr. Alwan Masih
General Secretary
Church of North India

Mr. Sudipta Singh
Director Programmes
Church of North India

Introduction

The Church of North India (CNI) was formed in 1970 when six denominations came together with the threefold aim of Unity, Witness and Service. The mandate of the church in the last 40 years of its existence has been to proclaim by word and deed the gospel of Jesus Christ, who is the Lord and Master of the Church for the salvation and good of all humankind through educational, medical, social, agricultural and other services, and also through worship and other activities of the Church which promote spiritual growth, self reliance, social justice and moral regeneration irrespective of caste, creed or color. However, the times and context within which the church exists have changed and are changing.

The Church needs to discern the signs of times. The great majority of our people are trapped in the socio economic globalised system which propagates poverty, environmental degradation, class, caste and gender bias and oppressive regimes. The earth we live in has become a heaven for a few and a hell for a majority of its inhabitants. A growth model showcased by globalization has led to resources being taken away from the poor towards the rich.

The dynamics of life are controlled by the market. The biodiversity, natural resources and human potential mostly remains unrealized to benefit the people within their own situations. More than 40% of the population of the region lives below poverty levels. Unjust distribution and increasing population are major contributors for poverty. Global forces see the region as an effective market in light of their interests and products. But this modernization benefits a mere handful of the population. This unjust system has led to violence and conflict within societies and communities on bases of ethnicity, caste and communal ideologies. Its evil effects can be seen in the growth of child labour, human trafficking and ecological exploitation.

There is a pervading sense of hopelessness and a fatalistic outlook to life. Thus we find armed conflicts on the rise. Terrorism, civil wars, political and communal violence, violation of human rights is the order of the day. The development model has become responsible for the marginalisation of dalits women and other indigenous groups. The sweeping changes in the economy and industrial policies are benefitting the urban areas only. Growth of multinationals and emphasis on foreign trade has not been conducive for a pattern of development that is oriented towards the basic needs of the poor. Women as a section face and fight multiple prejudices on account of culture, structures of patriarchy, traditions and unjust laws.

The crimes against nature have led to problems of soil erosion, deforestation, climate change, depletion of fish stocks and fresh water resources. The question we need to answer is "are we doing justice to the future generation if we continue to use all natural and non-renewable resources?" This environmental imbalance is directly affecting the lives of those who are dependent on it.

Our God is the God of Mission, because He constantly communicates with His creation, particularly human beings. Mission can be said to be God's activity where God is reconciling the world to Himself. The ultimate objective of this mission is to fulfill the promise of the scriptures of a new heaven and a new earth where there is harmony between God and His creation and virtues of the Kingdom of God exist hand in hand. (Ps: 87:7-13, Isa 11:1-9, 32:12-18, Rev. 21:1-2). The Church is called out by God to go into the world as His people and to bring the world to Himself. "For you are a people holy to the Lord your God, the Lord your God has chosen you to be the people of His own possession..." (Deut 7:6). Just as the Israelites were chosen to be a blessing unto all nations (Exod 19:6) so also the Church has been called to proclaim the good news and salvation of Christ, which they have received, to others. The Church of North India has journeyed forty years and labored in fulfilling this responsibility. But it is important to pause, look back, reflect, introspect past achievements, to identify the present challenges and to plan, formulate and envision the strategy and mission of the church for the future. The Church has journeyed thus far and been proud in its union of six different churches. But is that the Unity that we should continue to look towards today. If that is the unity we seek it would merely qualify as interdenominational unity. It would not be true "ecumenical" unity for ecumenical is also *oikoumene* which includes the whole inhabited earth.

The call for the Church is that God's people within need to come into unity to serve God's people on the periphery and those that are marginalized. The church needs to stand along with the people in their struggles and in solidarity with people's movement. The praxis of the pastoral care needs to be missiological and its perspectives need to change strategy focusing on communities beyond its four walls, communities that are broken and crying out for justice. It is when the church at all levels stands against the injustices inflicted upon fellow humans and the creation that the scriptures may be fulfilled that, "justice may roll down like waters and righteousness like an ever-flowing stream" (Amos 5:24).

The Structured Church needs to give way to a Serving Church, the church that is involved directly with the people on the model of Jesus. In Galatians 5:1 St.Paul says that "For Freedom Christ has set us free". Our freedom from the socio-political and economic hegemony has been through Christ and in our proclamation of Christ we need to make sure that this freedom is experienced by others.

The church needs to see that it reaches out to others in the name of Christ in a conscious, deliberate and consistent manner. The witness that the church requires today is that of the Crucified and Resurrected Christ. That it bears the marks of the Crucified Christ (1 Peter 2:21) and thereby is ready to suffer and struggle along with the people as a consequence of its participation in God's mission. The Church also needs to bear the mark of the Resurrected Christ (Phil 3:10) radiating hope to the hopeless and helpless.

The understanding of *diakonia, koinonia, kerygma, didache* and *liturgia* needs to be renewed in light of God's new mission and vision for the Church. For without serving others there can be no justice; without justice there can be no peace, without peace there can be no unity; and if the Church is not seen united with all those within its context there is no witness. Therefore, as we celebrate 40 years of our union and existence it is imperative that we bring various sections of people such as youth, women, lay people, clergies, bishops and leaders within the church together to redesign and revitalize our missional commitment and vision for the future.

An Executive Summary of the Mission Conference 2010

*Organized as part of Celebrations of 40 Years of Unity,
Witness and Service of Church of North India*

Being Thankful to God for Journeying With Us

Celebrations do not carry any meaning unless we are grateful to God! This was exclaimed and affirmed by the Most Rev. Dr. Purely Lyngdoh, during the inaugural worship to mark the opening of the Mission Conference organized as a part of celebrating four decades of the missional journey of the Church of North India at Shalom Hall, Hislop College, Nagpur on 12th October 2010 under the theme "People of God for All of God's People: Witnessing to Unity at the Service of Justice". This historical conference was attended by more than 500 people including Bishops, Clergies, Lay People, Women, Overseas Mission Partners and Ecumenical Leaders who have sojourned with the Church of North India in fulfilling its mission agenda through various ways and means.

Inaugurating the conference the Moderator of the Church of North India, The Most Rev. Dr. Purely Lyngdoh, shared a Biblical reflection appealing to the gathering to be thankful to God for His guiding and sustainable grace in the past years in which the church been shaped and strengthened to witness Christ through services and proclamation of justice. He based the reflection on Luke 17: 11 – 19 and said that God has bestowed us with innumerous blessings over the years in our socio-congregational lives, and many of the things that we have been able to do or achieve are possible because of our united concerted efforts. Therefore, we have to be thankful to God lest we be like the 10 lepers Jesus cleansed. They were told to go and show themselves to the priests and in obeying, heading out on the road to the priests, on the way, they were healed. Only one returned to give thanks to Jesus. Are we really thankful to God for being our sojourner in the past 40 years? Let this celebration be a time of thanksgiving.

People of God for all God's People: Witnessing to Unity at the Service of Justice

Rev. Dr. Roger Gaikwad, Principal of Aizawl Theological College, enthralled the delegates with his Mizo greeting 'cheebai' i.e. peace. In his keynote address on the given theme, he took the gathering 40 years back to the day when different churches had come together in one faith evolving into the Church of North India. He reminded that 40 years ago our pilgrimage started as united and uniting mission. He also underlined that along with CNI's 40 years completion, the year 2010 also marks the centenary of the Edinburg Conference in which mission mandate was globally revisited and reaffirmed. This is high time that we should remember that all people are equally significant in the sight of our Lord and we must also come together and bond with one another leaving our differences aside. We should not limit our bonding for programs and projects alone but also for the cause of justice. And this bonding would give rise to the movements from the local congregations. These movements shall be 'witness through unity'.

Discerning the Signs of the Time for Mission in the light of Accra Confession

Rev. Dn. Philip Peacock, Lecturer from Bishop's College, Kolkata screened a short film 'I am Dalit, How are you?' that highlighted the plights of dalits. In most parts of India, dalits are still treated as untouchables and are forced to do lowly work like scavenging, cleaning and disposing human excreta. In his presentation, he asserted that justice lay at the very heart of God, that the Biblical God was a God of justice and that this demanded that the Church not only involve in ethical acts of justice but also that it grow into the understanding that doing justice was integral to faith itself. He also asserted that unity was critical to the church and that the church looks not only at denominational unity but also struggle for social, political and economic inequality that meant overcoming the sins of caste and patriarchy. He further called the church into solidarity with the poor and struggling communities as its missiological commitment. His paper expounded on putting Jesus at the heart of faith in relation to Accra Confession from Asian Perspective. It was important that we as the Church of North India, after 40 years of union reflected on what this confession means for us a church in the Asian context.

Affirming Unity Proclaiming Justice as Exploring a New Mission Agenda in a Fractured World

Leading to outline the agenda of the church for the coming years the Rt. Rev. S. R. Cutting, bishop of Diocese of Agra, said that the CNI believes in Jesus' Nazareth Manifesto (Luke 4:16-18) as the declaration of Jesus' Mission on earth. Therefore, the Church's mission is the same as Jesus' mission because Jesus is the Head of the Church and the Church is his body carrying on His mission on earth. Proclaiming justice as an essential part of the mission is part of Nazareth manifesto. So the Church gets involved in the struggles of the people for justice.

"The Church of North India needs to respond to many challenges by committing herself to decisive action. If this opportunity to act is missed or allowed to pass by, the loss for the Church in India, for the Gospel, and for all the people of this nation will be immeasurable" said Rev. Dr. (habil) James Massey while spelling out the mission agenda of the church in a fractured world. He further added that "Jesus wept over Jerusalem due to its people's inability to perceive their Kairos. Will the Indian Church be able to perceive her Kairos that is at hand? As far as the Church of North India is concerned she has done well in this direction up till now as we have seen in the story of the development of her mission concept; but now the time (Kairos) has come for her to go for all out action, based on a well-planned road map to implement the God-given agenda to us."

Continuing with the same line of thoughts Ms. Sadhona Ganguli, a former National General Secretary of YWCA, stated that peoples struggle for human dignity and justice is the vision of the ministry of the church as envisaged in the plan of union of the CNI. Yet as a movement we have not fully utilized our united strength to realize measurable goals. She further said that every congregation should have a strong partnership of men and women for nurturing spiritual growth and positive values within its membership of families.

Healing a Broken World: Pastoral Perspective on Missiological Praxis

Mr. Philip Jadhav, former General Secretary of YMCA, New Delhi, presently the Chairman of the Delhi Forum, New Delhi dealt with "Healing a Broken World: Pastoral Perspective on Missiological Praxis". In his presentation he stated that among the community of nation states, India is generally projected as a fast emerging economic power. But contrast realities show that 80% of Indians live on ₹25 per day. India also adapted the policy of liberalisation, privatisation and globalisation. This has led to exploitation of natural resources for Growth Oriented Development. India he said also faces issues of environmental degradation and displacement of people. The social realities experienced by the people today are direct consequences of unjust and exploitative social and economic systems. To evolve pro-life and pro-people governance systems and structures, all people of God, the Church, has to be mobilized to join the movement to stop destructive forces and encourage, support and strengthen initiatives working on alternative models of development.

Unity for Justice: New ecumenical perspective for the future

The Rev Dr. Richard W Fee, General Secretary, Presbyterian Church of Canada, spoke on the topic, "Unity for Justice: new ecumenical perspective for the future." He said that there is an English expression, "if it isn't broken then don't fix it" which is applicable to the discussion of unity, justice and ecumenical perspective. He said that, "our theme challenges us to the roots of our faith". Quoting Mahatma Gandhi's seven deadly Social Sins which speak of the brokenness in human relations, the things that separate and the things that rent asunder true unity in our social interactions. A reminder for all of us of what he said is very pertinent and apt.

In line with the same subtheme Rev. Dr. Vinita Eusebius spoke about the children at risk, economic injustice, poverty, globalization, climate injustice and emphasized on gender justice. In her presentation she highlighted the causes and effects of injustice speaking on issues of children at risk, economic injustice leading to poverty, population growth especially in Indian context, Health Issues, Globalization, patriarchy and gender injustice, education and climate injustice and environmental degradation. Putting into perspective the mission of the church she said that God in Christ calls us to be involved in His Mission and purpose in the world. The journey for justice therefore is to move on as one people in our pilgrimage with God and for the people. There is an urgent need to review and evaluate the methods and impact of the traditional mission practices and seriously make advancements to promote holistic mission in the context of South Asian plurality, poverty and injustice. Rev. Dr. Eusebius challenged the participants to be an alternative community, resisting the prevailing ethos of making profits at any cost and subscribing to a different lifestyle and value system.

Serving Justice: Rethinking Diakonia from the Perspective of the Marginalized

Rev. Dr. R. Daniel Premkumar, Director Designate, Board of Diaconal Services, Church of South India, spoke about the acts of justice as fruits of righteousness: biblical overtures like the miserable Kick-off for an all time Grand Mission Paradigm and locate energy for mission tucked away in parishes. He challenged the Church of North India's visions beyond forty whether it is ready to encounter contentious issues? Why not join-in the Emmaus Walk? Can Church boldly address issues which are deep rooted and seemingly invincible?

Dr. Shailendra Awale, Chief Functionary/Secretary, CNI Synodical Board of Social Services, spoke with empathy about the marginalized people and their sufferings. Talking on the pathos of these marginalized communities Dr. Awale shared from his personal experiences how his

Bengali-speaking maid was forcefully displaced by the system. Not only her but other Bengali families too especially Muslims suffered this fate as the system thought of them as threat to the nation! These were the same poor families who toiled hard on meager wages, laboring day and night to 'shine' our India. He urged the gathering to move ahead from the charity to rights-based approach and be in solidarity with these brethren by experiencing their pain. This samvedana empathy shall instill the feeling in us that our dalit and adivasi brethren are too created in the image of our God and they too deserve the benefits we are enjoying alone.

Conclusion

The members got into groups to discuss on the issues that emerged from the different speakers to concretize a programmatic road map for the future mission engagement of the church in Indian context. All these talks have helped the Church of North India in formulating its missional road map for the years to come affirming that affirm that "our response to a God of justice, that our faith in Jesus who calls us to be one, and the work of the Holy Spirit who grieves when people are divided, demands that we recommit ourselves to solidarity with Dalits, adivasis and tribals and the empowerment of women. This is very clear from the Mission Commitment declared by the delegates.

Mission Commitment

We, the laity, women, theologians, pastors and Bishops of the Church of North India gathered in Nagpur on the 12th and the 13th of October 2010 to celebrate forty years of our union and existence. As we celebrated our unity we also endeavored to rediscover for ourselves the meaning of unity in the twenty first century and to revision its missiological implications.

Inspired by different thematic presentations that were made around the theme People of God for all God's People: Witnessing to unity at the service of justice, we rejoiced in the vision of our foremothers and forefathers of faith who forty years ago named the sin of disunity and denominational division and in response to the call of Jesus, that the Church be one (John 17:21), overcame their differences and divisions to form the Church of North India. We understand however, that our unity is not uniformity, we acknowledge and affirm the richness of our diversity, we are one but we are not the same.

While we celebrate our common unity that is expressed in our common worship and in our common mission towards working among the marginalized and dispossessed, we also recognized that being a united and uniting church implies that we continue to name the sin of disunity among us even today. We named the sin of caste and patriarchy that continues to divide our church.

We affirm that our response to a God of justice, that our faith in Jesus who calls us to be one, and the work of the Holy Spirit who grieves when the people of God are divided, demands that we recommit ourselves to solidarity with Dalits, adivasis and tribals and the empowerment of women. We are committed to working with children as being integral to our understanding of both ministry and mission.

We furthered our commitment to being one church and saw engagement with the world for the sake of justice as being the mission of the church in the world. We affirm that the congregation should be in the forefront of this mission. We affirm that perceiving the congregation as the locus from which mission is done requires both the decentralization of hierarchical power and authority to rediscover the congregations as places of healing as well as the empowerment of the congregation for spiritual renewal that is directed towards holistic transformation both within as well as outside of the church. We affirm that this renewal of congregations should be through a continuing programme of contextually relevant theological education for both clergy as well as laity. We therefore commit to the development of theologies, liturgies and lectionaries that are both rooted in the life of the worshipping community as well as directed towards the service of the marginalized. We acknowledge that we live in a broken world and we commit to working towards a mission and ministry of reconciliation and healing.

We affirm that children are central to the life of a vibrant, concerned, worshipping community and therefore we should work towards developing Sunday School Syllabi that is pertinent to the Church of North India.

We understand that being a church that is committed to a transformative mission requires resources. We see the urgent need for the membership of the Church of North India to commit to regular tithing so that we can move towards self- reliance. We commit to transparency and accountability at all levels of Church administration and governance. We also see the sharing of resources as being central to unity and looked forward to a time when this could be expressed at all levels of administration in the Church of North India.

We are a people who have journeyed together for forty years; we testify that God has been our guide and our fellow traveler. We look forward to our jubilee in hope and anticipation of God's continuing journey with us, the people of God, committed to all of God's people.

Delegates
Mission Conference 2010, Nagpur
Church of North India

People of God for All of God's People: Witnessing to Unity at the Service of Justice

– Roger Gaikwad

We are gathered here in Nagpur at a very significant time in history. As the Church of North India we started our pilgrimage as a united and uniting church in this very city 40 years ago having Unity-Witness-Service as its life-guiding motto. In this very year we are celebrating the centenary of the World Missionary Conference held in Edinburgh, which strengthened the foundations of world-wide ecumenical togetherness in mission. This ecumenism arose out of a zealous commitment to the motto, "Evangelization of the World in This Generation." In celebrating these two epochal events, we have organized this Mission Conference through the course of which we seek to honor and learn from the past as well as envision the future. This conference is not taking place in a vacuum or any idyllic setting. Mr. Alwan Masih, the new General Secretary of the CNI, articulates the context in which we are meeting: "We recognize that we are meeting at a time when the world has been plunged into global economic crisis imposing a crushing burden on the poor and those at the margin, escalating violence and terrorism, making everyone cry for peace, a time of unprecedented pressures on subaltern communities to fight to preserve their very survival and identity, of unjustifiable marginalisation and oppression of women and children, and raging violence."[1] Given such a context, what would be the "Vision beyond 40" for the Church of North India?

Biblically speaking, "forty years" is a very symbolic period. It is the period of the journey of the Hebrew people beginning with the Exodus from Egypt and culminating in their entry to Canaan, the Promised Land. The forty years constituted the formative stage of the Israelites as "People of God". God participated in the lives of the people throughout this period. The Exodus event itself was made possible by divine intervention, with Moses being his chief instrument. As per popular biblical tradition, these Hebrews were a united and uniting body of tribes, whom God delivered out of Egyptian bondage, and commissioned to become a people of God for God's purposes: "You have seen what I did to the Egyptians, and how I bore you on eagles' wings and brought you to myself. Now therefore, if you will obey my voice and keep my covenant, you shall be my own possession among all peoples... and you shall be to me a kingdom of priests and a holy nation" (Ex.19:4-6). Thereafter on Mount Sinai, God delivered the Ten Commandments to the people. These foundational Ten Commandments were followed by the laying down of rules and regulations for responsible communitarian living. Then came the making of the holy tabernacle and the consecration of the priests. As the story of the journeying people of God continues to unfold, they encounter intra-community and inter-community problems. These problems test their faith in God and their commitment to God's purposes. At times they were even tempted to back to Egypt. One also notices that they tended to become self-centered as a community. An important component of the original call, as given by God to Abraham, "... by you all the families of the earth shall bless themselves" (Gen. 12:3), seems to have been neglected; the Israelites held on to the first part of that component, "I will bless those who bless you, and him who curses you, I will curse." The people of God

---

[1] Extracted from the Letter of Invitation to participate in the present Mission Conference.

were yet to realize their calling to be a blessing to all of God's people. While they were proud of the privilege that they were People of God, they were yet to realize the implications of this privilege: being together not only among themselves, but being together (united) in solidarity with all peoples of the world who were yoked to different bondages, sharing (witnessing) the experience of the liberating God, and participating (serving) in the fulfillment of God's vision of leading all to the land flowing with milk and honey.

Forty years ago, the Church of North India came into existence in Nagpur. As we are all aware, six churches formed the CNI: the Council of Baptist Churches in Northern India, the Church of the Brethren, the Disciples of Christ, the Church of India (Anglican, formerly known as the Church of India, Pakistan, Burma and Ceylon), the Methodist Church (British and Australasian Conferences) and the United Church of Northern India. It wasn't as such an exodus from political and socio-economic slavery. However, it was an expression of exodus from the problems of denominationalism, which was weakening the life and testimony of the Church, particularly in North India:

> The concern for unity of the Church grew out of a zeal for the mission of the Church, because a divided Church could not bear witness to the one Gospel and the one Lord in a country like India with diverse religions, languages, races and cultures. Through the process of negotiations and prayerful seeking of the guidance of Holy Spirit unity was achieved in the understanding and practice of the sacraments of Baptism and the Lord's Supper, the three-fold ministry of Bishops, Presbyters and Deacons and in the organizational structures of Pastorates, Dioceses and the Synod, Episcopacy was received and accepted as both constitutional and historic. Provision has been made for diverse liturgical practices and understandings of the divine revelation, provided that these do not violate the basic Faith and Order of the Church or disrupt the unity and fellowship within the Church.[2]

Thus during the course of forty years, the Church of North India has evolved its constitution, it has shaped its dioceses, it has developed the Synod Secretariat, and it has engaged itself in different activities at the local, diocesan, and Synod level. It has drawn up a mission

---

[2] *http://www.cnisynod.org/beginning.aspx* (Downloaded on 08.10.10).

statement: "The Church of North India ... is committed to announce the Good News of the reign of God inaugurated through death and resurrection of Jesus Christ in proclamation and to demonstrate in actions to restore the integrity of God's creation through continuous struggle against the demonic powers by breaking down the barriers of caste, class, gender, economic inequality and exploitation of the nature."[3] It also drew up Mission Priorities for the first decade of the 21st century: Re-juvinating Pastoral Ministry; Evangelism within and without for costly discipleship; Re-structuring the structure; Ministry of Service; Solidarity with subaltern; Healing Communities; and Equipping God's People for Participatory Learning Process.[4] The Church has also gone through a process of evaluation. While there have been occasions of joyous celebration during the past 40 years, the Church has also faced several challenges. Are we ready for venturing into the future? In another 10 years time we will celebrate 50 years of our existence. (Then perhaps we shall all start talking about the 50th Jubilee Year as described in Leviticus 25 as the time for atonement, for recreation, economic reform and social reform). Yes, we shall continue to grow with chronological years and we shall continue to celebrate those chronological milestones. The call and commission given to us by God is to make those chronological celebrations as times of "kairos", of qualitative transformation in the Church, Society and all Creation. The "Land flowing with milk and honey" and the "Gospel of liberation and transformative holistic growth" (the Nazareth Manifesto as recorded in Luke 4:18-19) continue to be our guiding visional goals. Hence the importance of our theme for this Mission Conference: People of God for All of God's People: Witnessing to Unity at the Service of Justice.

It is significant that theme does not say "The People of God" but just "People of God". It cautions us against assuming any arrogant stance that we Christians alone are the people of God. In Isaiah 19: 24-25, the word of God declares: In that day *Israel will be the third with*

---

[3] *http://www.cnisynod.org* (Downloaded on 08.10.10).

[4] *http://www.cnisynod.org/mission.aspx* (Downloaded on 08.10.10).

Egypt and Assyria, a blessing in the midst of the earth. Whom the Lord of hosts has blessed, saying, "Blessed be *Egypt my people*, and *Assyria the work of my hands*, and Israel my heritage." (Emphasis added). Then again in Amos 9:7 it is written: "Are you not like the Ethiopians to me, O people of Israel?" says the Lord. "Did I not bring up Israel from the land of Egypt, and the Philistines from Caphtor and the Syrians from Kir?" God has indeed been participation in the histories of all nations. So each nation could in its own way consider itself as "People of God." As Christians we have experienced liberative salvation in relation to the "kingdom of God" in Jesus. And so Peter following the sense of calling which the Jews had, of being people of God, asserts, "You are a chosen race, a royal priesthood, a holy nation, God's own people that you may declare the wonderful deeds of him who called you out of darkness into his marvelous light." (1 Pet. 2: 9)

The second section of the theme when read with the first part emphasizes: People of God *for All of God's People.* This too is very significant. Chosenness or salvation is no private privilege. It is meant to share with others. The story in 2 Kgs chapter 7 narrates how when the people of Samaria were experiencing famine like conditions since the city was besieged by the enemy, four lepers go over to the camp of the enemy only to find it abandoned, but with food, livestock, clothes, silver and gold still lying around. The lepers were tempted to have it all for themselves, but then they said, "We are not doing right. This day is a day of good news; if we are silent and wait until morning light, punishment will overtake us; now therefore come let us go and tell the King's household." (2 Kgs.7:9). The gospel is for all! To paraphrase what D.T. Niles once said, mission is like one poor person telling another where to find bread. However while the gospel is for all, there is a preferential option for the least, the last and the lost, the people on the "margins'. This concern is clearly expressed by Jesus in the parable on the judgment, in Matthew 25:31-46. There it is mentioned that the King will say to those on his right hand, "Come O blessed of my Father, inherit the kingdom prepared for you from the foundation of the world; for I was hungry and you gave me food, I was thirsty and you gave me drink, I was a stranger and you welcomed me, I was sick and you visited me, I was in prison and you came to me."

Mission today however is not to be limited to charity. Charity in the sense of a ministry of compassion for those who are suffering because of the socio-economic, political, religio-cultural, technological-ecological structures of society, is important and needs to be carried on. However charity is not the solution to suffering in society. It does not change the unjust status quo in society. Therefore the theme of our conference emphasizes Justice. Forty years ago the Church of North India came into existence to remove the denominational divisions among churches. Today the call for the CNI is to work for the removal of unjust divisions in society be it of caste, of patriarchy, of globalization, and between humans and creation. Let us be remained of the words of Paul in Galatians 3:28 – "There is neither Jew nor Greek, there is neither slave nor free, there is neither male nor female; for you are all one in Christ Jesus." We should not be content with saying," There is neither Baptist, nor Anglican in Christ Jesus!" There is more to ecumenism and unity than mere denomination harmony and oneness.

How are we to engage ourselves in the mission of justice? The theme for our conference suggests: Witnessing to unity. This phrase emphasizes the importance of the bonding together of people for the cause of justice. It is not that we are not doing it. We have been engaged in it since the past 40 years. However in general our bonding together has been more in the sense of "programmes" and "projects" for which funds are available. Our programmes and projects need to become "movements", originating from the local congregations. The problem in the history of Christianity is that time and again the Jesus movement has grown into an organization. When any movement becomes an organization, with its institutions and funds it becomes 'successes-oriented. Therefore, now a day we look for management experts to run such organizations, and so more and more professionalism rather than the original vocation commitment, enters the organization. The programmes and projects no doubt serve a good purpose, but do they inspire and motivate the local congregations to pursue those programmes and projects as movements among themselves? The phrase "witnessing to unity" seems to imply that Christians need to make a show of oneness by committing themselves to the cause of justice. This show of oneness again implies that we have to work towards removal of all that divides us in the congregations. The Pentecost community model should stir us to work together in unity: "and all who believed were together and had all things in common.' (Acts. 2: 44).

I would have personally preferred the phrase "Witnessing through Unity". It is not merely a matter of making a show of unity. It is more a matter of bearing witness to the gospel of Jesus Christ through our being together in solidarity not only among ourselves as a religious community of Christians but among ourselves as human beings who are struggling yet challenged to bear witness to the gospel in Nagpur and Maharashtra, In North India, in South Asia and unto the ends of the earth.

Reflecting on Putting Justice at the Heart of Faith from an Asian Perspective

– Philip Vinod Peacock

Introduction

In our times, if there is one document, that calls us to place justice at the heart of faith, it is the Accra Confession. The Accra confession is an initiative which calls all those who are part of the Reformed Communion and churches outside of it as well to reflect on what it means to live faithfully as the disciples of Christ in our times and more specifically how do we respond to the nexus of economic, social, political and military power that has come to be defined as Empire. It is important that we as the Church of North India, after 40 years of union to reflect on what this confession means for us a church in the Asian context. At the outset itself I would like to place on record three factors that distinguishes Asia, from perhaps the two other regions that are making presentations today, with regards to the Accra confession.

Ambiguity

If one were to read the relevant literature there could no denying that Asia is an ambiguous continent. Geographically the boundaries of Asia remain ambiguous and several continue to debate whether or not

countries such as Russia and Turkey belong to Asia. Further, unlike
Europe that has constructed a history, with extremely violent
consequences, that have claimed a common cultural (and sometimes
racial) root, while at the same time accounting for difference, both
linguistic and cultural, Asia has not imagined such a past. Although,
and perhaps also because, Asia has played a pivotal role in the
European construction of itself, 'Asia', in the modern discourse has
been constructed as the ambiguous 'other', as perhaps Edward Said
would suggest. While I would not deny that this has also been the
experience of both Latin American and Africa, it has not happened to
the extent that it has in Asia. Moreover While there have been efforts
to create a pan-Asian identity politically, economically and perhaps
even within the context of theology, it is my assessment that these have
not succeeded in creating an 'Asian consciousness' as perhaps have
similar attempts within the context of Africa or South America.

Diversity

Related to the issue of Asian ambiguity is the experience of cultural,
ethnic and religious diversity. Asia is a continent that occupies around
30% of the land mass of the world and hosts around 60% of the world's
population that is extremely diverse culturally, ethnically, politically
and religiously.

There are a number of different ethnic groups that live within Asia,
like in other continents Asia has its own multiplicity of ethnic groups
that are further divided along lines of language and dialect. However
what is important to note is that because of the size and the population
of the continent, this diversity is probably more than elsewhere.
Likewise there is also a diversity of political systems and processes
that range from multi-party democracies on the one end to monarchies
and dictatorships on the other.

Culturally it is difficult to speak of an overarching Asian culture.
This is particularly true while speaking of traditional cultural practice,
food, myths, rituals etc. Within the context of Asia there lies an extreme
diversity of culture. Of course one must not exaggerate this cultural
diversity. Living in a globalized world it would be naïve to suggest
that there is little similarity between the culture of West Asia and East

Asia, for example. After all cultural globalization has meant the proliferation of homogenized cultural artefacts across the globe, Dubai does not look or act, or tries not to look or act any different from Seoul or Tokyo or even New York or Frankfurt for that matter. However what is important for us to note is that the elements of this homogenous culture are not essentially Asian but are reflective of a global market system which has become the driving force of culture today. Interestingly many of the cultural artefacts of modernity are literally produced in sweatshops around Asia.

Most importantly for our purposes however, is the multiplicity of religious expressions that are to be found in Asia. Asia is after all home to several major world religions. The list would include Hinduism, Jainism, Buddhism, Judaism, Christianity, Islam and Sikhism. This would perhaps take us to our last important factor, namely minority.

Minority

While Christianity was founded in Asia, and the name Christian first used in Asia, one would have to admit that the church in Asia is a minority. In most countries in Asia, Christianity is the minority religion which I believe is one important factor for us to consider when we speak of the significance of the Accra confession for Asia.

While one would acknowledge a wide diversity in Asia, I would believe that there is a certain commonality of experience among the people of Asia. We shall make some attempt to speak of the commonality of this experience by mapping the Asian context.

Mapping the Asian Context

The Struggle Against Colonialism

If there is a common experience in Asia it would probably lie in its experience of colonialism. Colonialism has had a deep and devastating impact on Asia the effects of which continue to be seen even today. While Asia and Europe probably began the transition into modernity at the same time, the both of them did this in entirely different ways, one as the colonizer and the other as the colonized. Colonialism impacted Asia economically, politically, socially and psychologically.

On the economic front colonialism meant nothing but the raw extraction from Asia for the wealth creation of the west. This extraction was devastating to local economies who, as a result of colonialism, were overturned to become producers of raw materials for consumers in Europe.

On the political front, for the colonized, colonialism meant the loss of the right to self-rule and self-determination. In the latter part of the nineteenth century and in the twentieth century the opposition to colonial imperialism took on the form of the rise of nationalism which attempted to confront empire using the western entity of the nation state. The process was not without its own issues and new studies on nationalism are discovering that it often served to crystallize the dominance of the local elite that colluded with colonial interests and colonial ideology for their own purposes even if they opposed colonial imperialism. The end of imperialism therefore for several powerless groups across Asia merely meant the handing over of reins to new masters.

On the social front what often happened was that the colonial powers colluded with local dominant communities that either served to ratify ancient hierarchies, re-create them in new ways or to create altogether new ones. Essentially colonialism meant that more vulnerable groups, particularly women, peasants, small artisans, indigenous people and those who lay on at the bottom of social hierarchies became even more vulnerable.

On the psychological front colonialism was constructed and imagined as a sense of loss, defeat and even emasculation of the colonized. Colonialism was after all not just the extraction of wealth but was also the contestation of ideas within which certain ideologies, scientific rationalism, for example were privileged over all others. This sense of loss and emasculation continues to exhibit itself in various ways including the glorification of violence, colonial constructions of knowledge and imagination of a glorious past that has its own problematic today. There is of course significant work being done by Asians today in the field of post-colonialism that is seeking to deconstruct some of this.

The Struggle Against Poverty

Another common experience across Asia would be the experience of poverty. In India, the country I come from, official statistics tell us that 29% of the population lie below the poverty line. The question however is how is that line drawn? What defines the poverty line? In India the poverty line is defined as the amount of money required to purchase 1200 calories of food - the minimum daily requirement of an adult. To put it in another way, in my country 29% of the population are starving. The numbers of those who are malnourished are far worse. Dietrich and Wielenga remind us that "Poverty is not just the lack of cash to buy minimum food but it manifests itself in malnutrition, poor environment (polluted air and water) poor clothing, poor housing or no housing at all, lack of space, poor health, poor education and so on. Poverty means hunger, disease and despair. It means children dying of malnutrition. It means child labour, bonded labour and unhealthy work at low wages. It means dependency and abuse. It means the break up of families in search of work."

It would be naïve for us to suggest that poverty in Asia is the result of colonialism; such a view is too simplistic and mono-causal. However what we must also realize is that the logic of the present economic order that places value on profit over people has only served to worsen poverty. The situation is made worse by state and non-state actors such as international financial bodies and Transnational Corporations pressing for a particular economic model that would benefit the powerful but would wreak havoc on the lives of the powerless. This neo-liberal agenda is being pushed through structural adjustment programmes that seek to privatize, liberalize and globalize the economy subsuming all things to the logic of profit making. Unemployment, reduction of workers' rights and the increasing gap between the rich and the poor is the result of this.

Curiously capitalism has taken on two specific forms in Asia, the first is what can be referred to as authoritarian capitalism, where through state interference a capitalistic agenda is being pushed. This either takes the extreme form of China who pushes the agenda of capitalism with military power, or the example of India where the state openly acts in favour of the corporations and against the rights of the people as has been amply been witnessed to in the recent ruling in the Bhopal Gas Tragedy case as well as in the Vedanta and POSCO corporations case in Orissa in India. Interestingly capitalism envisages the reduction of the role of the state leaving the economic system to the invisible hand.

The second form of Capitalism found in Asia is what Naomi Klein would refer to as disaster capitalism where corporations and governments move into areas devastated by natural or human made calamities to introduce a neo-liberal agenda. Examples of this can be witnessed to in the war torn areas of Iraq and Afghanistan or in the Tsunami struck areas of Indonesia or Sri Lanka!

The Struggle Against Environmental Degradation

Linked to the struggle against poverty is also the struggle against environmental degradation. Reliance on a growth based economic system has meant an increasing pressure on the environment. Climate change has affected several parts of Asia in different ways including increasingly extreme weather, floods and drought, loss of species and rising sea levels. While the debate between the developed and developing countries of the world continue over carbon emissions, fact is that Asia has not only suffered because of climate change but in as much as it also continues with its economies of phenomenal growth it also continues to contribute to the problem!

The Struggle Against Violence

Another common feature that can be found around Asia is the level of violence. Whether it is war, armed conflict, state violence, terrorism, insurgency movements, human rights violations, structural violence or gender-based violence, violence is endemic in Asia. Of particular significance for Asia is religious violence, whether it is between sects of the same religion or between two religious groups.

The Struggle Against Internal Hierarchies

While we speak of the context of Asia we must also not forget the presence of internal hierarchies that exist among Asian communities.

Structures like caste and patriarchy continue to discriminate against and cause violence towards millions of Asians.

While we have looked at the Asian context by raising several specific issues it is important for us to note the connections that exist between these various elements, all of them working together in certain places to further the systems of injustice that exist. In the next section we shall be looking at the relevance of the Accra confession for Asia

Relevance of the Accra Confession for Asia

It is important for us to note that there were several Asians who were involved with the process of covenanting for justice in the economy and in the earth and they have obviously brought their contextual experience into the production of this document. There are some specific ways however, in which the Accra Confession relates to Asia.

Calling the Faithful to Engage with the World

Firstly the Accra Confession is a call to the faithful to engage with the world, this has been the legacy of both Calvin and the reformed tradition! Calvin himself wrote much about the economic system of his time indicating to us that the economy serve human interests and particularly the interests of the poor. The legacy of Calvin in the present time should encourage us to engage with economic systems contextually and pastorally from the perspective of justice ensuring that our economies serve the interests of people and not the large multinational companies.

In the Asian context however the gospel came to the people as part of the colonial enterprise and was in many ways used as a tool of subjugation. In this sense the gospel that was presented was a depoliticised gospel that called people to disengage with the world and not question the violence of the system. Therefore an otherworldly faith was encouraged and cultivated. This understanding of the gospel still continues in Asia with many believing that being a believer necessitates withdrawal from the world.

The relevance of the Accra Confession however is to call the attention of the faithful to the real crisis of the world and sees engagement with it as the legitimate act of faith. It calls the believer to understand that justice is the very substance of faith. And this takes us to our second point that the Accra confession calls Asian Christians to faith based stands for justice.

The Accra Confession Calls Asian Christians to Faith Based Stands for Justice
For Asian Christians justice is very often reduced to a question of ethics. Acts of justice are seen as what one should do because one is a Christian. Therefore it is not uncommon for Asian Christians to get involved with charity work. Several churches take on many different projects in which they try to find the right thing to do. The Accra confession however calls Asian Christians to understand that justice is a matter of faith, it is a matter of confession. It is the very heart of God. To put it in other words, it is not Christians who should be involved with acts of justice, rather it is doing acts of justice that make us Christian as the Accra confession puts it "Speaking from our Reformed tradition and having read the signs of the times, the General Council of the World Alliance of Reformed Churches affirms that global economic justice is essential to the integrity of our faith in God and our discipleship as Christians. We believe that the integrity of our faith is at stake if we remain silent or refuse to act in the face of the current system of neoliberal economic globalization and therefore we confess before God and one another."

The Relevance of Speaking the Language of Empire
While there has been considerable debate about the use and the meaning of the word Empire in the Accra Confession, this is probably the part that has endeared Asians, both Christians and those belonging to other faiths to it. Having been brutalised by colonialism and neo-colonialism, Asians have a real experience of what Empire is. Many Asians see the word Empire as a legitimate nomenclature for all that has been destroying their lives, livelihood, community and environment. However Asians also realize that in the modern world Empire cannot be embodied by a single nation, however powerful. The feature of modernity is that power cannot be found in individuals or organizations, but rather in systems. Asians would define Empire as systems that accumulate power to serve the interests of a few at the

cost of many, as greatly increased distance between those who make the decisions and those who have to suffer them.

While we have spoken about how Christians in Asia are a minority, what we should also mention here is that in many countries in Asia they are the powerless minority. Christians in Asia are poor, dispossessed, women, Dalits, Minjung, Indigenous. They are not the ones who discern the signs of the times, they are those who experience them. They are the voices that the Accra confession calls us to hear. It is Asian Christians, whether it is the sweatshop worker in Indonesia, the sweeper in Pakistan, the Dalit in India, the indigenous person in the Philippines... who have experienced the violence of Empire. This document speaks of our experience; it calls us to live our faith in new ways.

Having said that however, perhaps what the Accra confession does not pay adequate attention to, is the reality of religious pluralism. While it is necessary for us to speak of justice as being a matter of faith for those of us in Asia that live in a multi-religious context, we cannot reduce justice to being a Christian project. The difficulties of seeing justice as a matter of faith is that it becomes a barrier to joining hands with secular movements for justice, and if we are to create another world then this joining of hands is a necessity. The need for us in Asia is also to open up spaces by which we can relate to other faiths and work together for the sake of justice, and maybe the Accra confession does not offer such spaces. Or perhaps, that we need to work creatively with the text so that it does.

Asian Churches and Accra Confession

Lastly we should consider how the churches in Asia have responded to the Accra confession. Immediately after the General Council, the Accra confession was circulated to Churches and seminaries in Asia for reflection and discussion. I myself remember being part of such a discussion in my seminary.

In fact just the day before I left for the US I was a resource person in a pastor's conference that was organized by the Council for World Mission, South Asian Region that was based on the Accra Confession and had as its theme, "Justice at the heart of faith". The conference invited Pastors from all the church traditions in South Asia including the Anglicans, the Baptists and the Reformed Orthodox churches, along with churches that have roots in the reformed tradition. The conference has the expected outcome of getting the participants to commit to the Accra confession and to discover how to proceed with this perspective. The Church of North India intends to begin from this year onwards an entire process on covenanting for justice in the economy and the earth, the dynamics of which are presently being worked out.

Yet there is work to be done, the Accra confession must filter down to the level of the local congregations that should begin to reflect on it and see how they can delegitimise Empire and work towards a just world which promises fullness of life for all.

Affirming Unity, Proclaiming Justice

Exploring a New Mission Agenda in a Fractured World

— James Massey

I. Introduction: United for Mission

In the course of the history of churches in India, we find that three united churches came into being at different stages: the United Church of North India (UCNI) in 1924, The Church of South India (CSI) in 1947, and the Church of North India (CNI) in 1970. However, if we take a look at the period prior to it, we find that division of churches had been worrying the church leaders from early point in time: in 1919 in one of the important conferences at Tranquebar (South India) this concern was clearly voiced when they lamented 'the tragedy and sin of divisions in this land'. These leaders feared that such divisions would 'hinder' the carrying out of the Christian witness/mission in the right spirit. Fifty years later this apprehension was again reflected in the pre-union document of CNI entitled *Forward to Union – The Church of North India* (1968), which reads as: "We have seen that, if God so wills, the Church of North India be both a continuation of the best that each negotiating Church has to bring into Union and a new creation in Christ transcending denominational division and revealing more clearly the unity that she intends for her people." These views were aired emphatically and clearly again later in the document: "Yet confronted by such an overwhelming responsibility, we find ourselves rendered weak and relatively impotent by our unhappy divisions for which we were not responsible and which have been, as it were, imposed upon us from without."[1] These two statements unmistakably point to us to 'affirm our unity', without which it would be impossible to carry out our 'mission'.

The second part of the topic of this paper is about 'proclaiming justice' which in fact needs us to define the 'mission agenda' of the Church. For this I shall once again like to go to the pre-union document *Forward to Union – The Church of North India* which also asks the same question: "What is the mission (or task) to which this new united Church is called and what does the Plan of Union provide in the way of guidelines to the Church in carrying out its mission?" It is interesting to note that in her forty-years journey, the Church of North India has made number of attempts to understand the nature of her mission, and consequently achieved an understanding in this regard. We shall trace this course of CNI attempts in the next section of this paper. However, I shall like to observe that the question about the 'mission agenda' which is raised directly here had been addressed by CNI on other occasion in different form. CNI consultation on "Towards a Holistic Understanding of Mission" (THUM) in July 1993 not only defined the mission but also had gone further saying: "This holistic understanding of Mission of mission must be translated into meaningful programme within the life of the Church. Despite the majority of the membership of church consisting of the marginalized, it has been primarily serving the interest of the elite and upper ten through educational, medical, and other institutions...."[2] While the first part of this statement relates to the need of relevant mission programme, the second part delves into the question of 'justice' to the 'majority'. By doing this the Church has evidently accepted that her mission till now had been limited to the 'elite and upper ten', which put the whole mission of the Church in question raising doubt about the direction in which not only CNI but even other Churches in India are going. This point incidentally also justifies the sub-theme of this paper i.e. "Exploring a new Mission Agenda in a Fractured World".

Before getting on with the discussion I would also like to refer to two world conferences held in Edinburgh: in 1910 and in 2010, which cover a hundred year journey of doing mission by the world Christianity. Edinburgh 1910 based upon "A Vision of Earth: - as one world, waiting, surely... bringing its one human race into one Catholic Church, through the message of the 'one Body, and one Spirit, one Lord, one Faith, one Baptism, one God and Father of all, who is over all, and through all, and in all'. Such was the vision which called together the World Missionary Conference of 1910."[3] Emphasis here was on 'proclaiming' that "Christianity - the religion of the light of the World - can ignore no light, however 'broken'; it must take them all into account, absorb them all into its central glow..." In this way 'by going into all the worlds', Christ's Church may recover "all the Light that is in Christ, become, like the Head, as it is His will she would become."[4] This emphasis after Edinburgh 1910 continued in different forms in 'mission' work in various regions of the world. The International Missionary Council's meeting at Tambaram, Madras, India (1938) also considers it.

As a departure from its stand of Edinburgh 1910, the 2010 moved from "A Church-centered mission to a mission-centered Church and towards an exploration of missionary collaboration beyond the Church".[5] Edinburgh 2010, while talking about 'Mission and Unity' refers to a bold vision of the 'unity' and its relationship with the mission. In this regard it says, "The ecumenical debate on evangelism has reminded us that we cannot allow a false dichotomy to be created as we play out truth and unity, prophetic witness for the values of the Kingdom of God, and vocation for the unity and Church. Therefore, ecumenical does not mean unity at any price, but is about costly unity for prophetic witness."[6]

It is this 'costly unity for prophetic witness' that will lead us in the remaining discussion of this paper, and which, I believe, should be the core of Christian 'mission' in the 'fractured world' of today. For convenience I shall divide the rest of my discussion under the following sub-heads:

- The case history of mission development of the Church of North India

- Prophetic witness which directs our future 'Mission Agenda'

- Conclusion: The God-given Mission Agenda for the Church.

II. The Case History of Mission Development of the Church of North India

The Church of North India in its present form was born on November 29, 1970. But the history of the development of her mission began even before her birth, because the mission concern had always been one of the main priorities before the members of the negotiating Churches. Later also, after the establishment of CNI, this continued as its major concern. Let us take a quick look at a few of the most important landmarks of the mission-development for our reflection.

The Church document known as *Plan of Church Union in North India and Pakistan;* (1965), served as the basis for union of six negotiating churches of North India, and helped in laying the foundation for the mission of the future United Church, that was to be called the Church of North India (CNI) in due course. This can be considered, therefore, as the first landmark in the process of developing CNI mission. The following excerpts from this document make this point clear: "To the whole Church and to every member of it belongs the duty and the privilege of spreading the good news of the Kingdom of God, and the message of salvation through Jesus Christ.. It is recognized as the contribution of members to the Church's work for the redemption of the whole life of man. . . By the life and witness of members in their daily contact with the world, lie the Church's evangelism tasks and opportunity; ... By sharing in the Church's corporate acts of witness and service; . . . By the full time service of the Church in the ministries of evangelism, education, healing and other forms of Christian service."[7]

The second landmark of the mission development of the Church of North India was an important Consultation held in November 1978 on the theme *"Churches' role in Social Service and Development"* under the auspices of the Synodical Board of Social Service of the Church of North India. This Consultation helped the Church to clear her understanding about her social concerns which in fact is a part of her mission. The Report of the Consultation says: "The objectives of the Churches' Social Concern is that (together) we may be partakers in and through Christ of God's creature and redemptive love in fulfilling His purpose for the World. This might be better expressed/carried out, in Him; our Lord's proclamation of His ministry as found in Luke 4:18 and 19."[8]

The next important landmark was a three years' Leadership Development Programme of the Church of North India entitled *Transfer of Vision*, which began immediately after the 5" Synod (November 1983) and continued till September 1986. This programme was comprehensive as well as intensive in nature and it could cover about 7000 leaders in the Church. One of the main thrust was to convey to these budding leaders the nature of the mission of the Church, which was stated in these words: "Deepening acquaintance transcending all barriers for proper emotional integration based on our common understanding of the Mission of the Church/local congregations and its related social service institutions that we have inherited, with a view to consolidate our efforts and initiatives as agents of change of iii the general socio-economic and political context of our country and to fix appropriate goals and priorities for our task ahead."[9]

The next most important landmark in the mission development of CNI was a programme knows as *"Towards a Holistic Understanding of Mission"* (THUM). The programme carried on for 30 months (from July 1993 to December 1995). The main thrust of the programme was to develop in the Church a holistic understanding of mission and priorities of the Church of North India. About the impact of the THUM, the 9th Synod made the following observation: "THUM had initiated a dynamic participatory process in the Church of North India involving all the members of the Church at congregational, diocesan and synodical levels in serious commitment to 're-working', re-visioning' and re-inventing' the concept of the Church and Mission. The Synod noted that the process had contributed to a holistic renewal, unity, witness and services of the Church. This process would need to be sustained and continued through appropriate CNI mechanism.'[10]

Based upon the strong recommendations of THUM, the Synod created the present 'CNI Commission on Mission' in 1995 with the following duties and functions and mandate: "I. It shall guide the Church in its thinking and formulations on God's mission and all issues and matters related to mission and evangelization taking into account the contemporary context. II. It shall initiate, co-ordinate, promote and guide thinking and action in mission and evangelization and shall mobilize human and material resource in the CNI for mission and evangelization. III. It shall perform all duties and functions that have been assigned to the Synod's Standing Committee called Christian Life. Mission and Evangelism Committee... IV. It shall deal with all mission concerns of the CNI on behalf of the Synod and shall be accountable to the Synod and its Executive Committee from time to time."[11]

The efforts of the 'CNI Commission on Mission' continued to assist the Church in defining her mission and it presented a draft 'Mission Statement' to the 11th Ordinary Meeting of the Synod of CNI during October 2001, which the Synod approved and adopted unanimously. This 'Mission Statement' of CNI reads as:

> The Church of North India as a United and Uniting together is committed to announce the Good news of the region of God inaugurated through death and resurrection of Jesus Christ in proclamation and to demonstrate in actions to restore the integrity of God's creation through continues struggle against the demonic powers by breaking down the harriers of caste, class, gender, economic inequality and exploitation of the nature.[12]

This in brief is the story of the Mission Development of the Church of North India. The main point to be noted here is that the mission of the Church actually belongs to her Lord, who further handed it to the whole Church in order to "work for the redemption of the whole life of man", as it was stated in the 'Plan of Church Union'. Also the process, which has already begun through the holistic understanding of God's mission, is meant for the continuing renewal, unity, witness and the service of the Church. But what actually is the nature of Christian mission or how the Church of North India finally has understood it? This question is answered in the report of THUM Consultation of 1993 in these words: "Holistic Mission means that the entire Church, Faith and Order, Life and Mission and Church organisations are united, willing and geared to be concerned about all human beings and each human being in his or her totality. Since the system and structures continue to dominate our lives, the Church's authentic Mission is to struggle against such structures and systems which oppress human beings."[13] Now, if this is what the Church means from her authentic Mission, then it has to work to "liberate" and "empower" the Dalits or tribals and other weaker sections of our society. In the same statement, the Church of North India even accepted the truth, where she has gone wrong in the past in carrying on her mission task. In this regard the THUM statement says, "This holistic understanding of mission must be translated into meaningful programmes within the life of the Church. Despite the majority of the membership of the Church consisting of the marginalised, it has been primarily serving the interest of the elite and upper ten through the educational, medical and other institutions..."[14] These two statements, represent the core of the understanding of the Church of her mission, which has to be holistic in nature involved in the service of "all human beings and each being in his or her totality." In order to fulfill it, the Church has to continue her struggle against those "structures and systems which oppress human beings." This indeed will be a proof of her "authentic mission" and this point leads us to the discussion of Biblical understanding of the 'Prophetic Witness'.

III. Prophetic Witness which Directs or Future 'Mission Agenda'

Prophetic traditions in the Bible are supposed to be the backbone of the Christian mission in this world. Three case histories of the early prophets as described in the first and second Samuel are earliest proofs of this claim. First prophet is an 'unnamed prophet', who brought the message of Lord God to the chief priest Eli whose sons had became corrupt in every sense. The unnamed prophet not only 'denounced' their evil works, but also made clear how God was going to punish his family by changing the established religious traditions of priesthood (1 Sam 2: 22-36). The second case history is of Prophet Nathan, who brought the divine message to King David - the most powerful political authority of his days. King David not only had raped the wife of one of his soldiers named Uriah the Hittite, but also had got him killed in a war. Prophet Nathan frankly and boldly told the King that it was "You" who committed the sin, as a result of which he shall have to face the divine punishment (2 Sam. 11:1-27, 12:1-15). The third case history is of Prophet Gad, who also announced the divine punishment for King David who had shown the weakness of his faith by taking stock of his armed forces in order to ascertain his military power (2 Sam. 24: 1-25).

The later prophets in the Bible also proclaimed the 'will' of God to the people of Israel at different periods. For example prophet Isaiah addressed them as Unfruitful Vineyard (church). He said:

> For the Vineyard of the Lord of hosts is the hour of Israel, and the people of Judah are his pleasant planting; he expected justice, but saw bloodshed; righteousness, but heard a cry! (Is 5:7)

The author of Isaiah in 'the Song of the Unfruitful Vineyard' narrated the condition of the people of Israel and Judah, and told them how they had invited the Lord's punishment on themselves by practicing 'social injustice' in various forms, which included amassing of property at the expense of others (Is 5: 8-10); drink and debauchery (Is 5:11) and lack of knowledge of their faith (Is. 5:13). Finally after denouncing these evils, which had become the part of his people's life, the prophet announced the Lord's Judgment on them (Isa. 5: 14-17). The most important verse of the song tells us that the basis of God's Judgment was "justice" and "righteousness" (Isa. 5: 16). This point is stressed by other prophets as well (Mic. 2; 1-6, Ezek. 45:11, Am. 6: 4-7). At another place Isaiah again proclaimed on behalf of the Lord that 'justice' and 'righteousness' were the criteria to determine whether one's faith was built on God's firm foundation or not (Isa. 28: 17).

Amos was also one of the prophets who spoke directly about 'justice' and 'righteousness'. For example at one place he addressed the people of Israel saying:

> Ah, you turn justice to wormwood, and bring righteousness to the ground! (Am. 5:7)

He continued to address God's people demanding from them to:

> "... let justice roll down like waters, and righteous like an ever-flowing stream". (Am. 5:14)

'Justice' means the establishment of the right, through fair legal procedures (Am. 5:15; Deut. 25:3), in accordance with the will of the Lord. And 'righteousness' means the quality of life in relationship to others in the community that gives rise to justice. Like Amos, prophet Micah also summed up the definition of true religion in the prophetic teaching, while challenging the people of Israel in the following words.

> He has told you, O mortal, what is good; and what does the Lord require of you but to do justice, and to love kindness, and to walk humbly with your God? (Mic 6: 8)

In continuing the prophetic traditions of the Old Testaments, in the New Testament too the prophet of the prophets, our Lord Jesus Christ, rebuked and denounced religious leaders of his days by saying:

> Woe to you, scribes and Pharisees hypocrites! For you tithe mint, dill, and cumin,

> And have neglected the weightier matters of law: Justice and mercy and faith. You blind guides! You strain out a gnat but Swallow a camel! (Mt.23: 23-24)

'Tithe' represents the tenth of agricultural produce given to support the temple and its priests (Lev. 27, 30-33, Num. 18: 8-32, Deut. 25: 1-5). 'Gnat' is an unclean insect (Lev. 11: 41-44) that was avoided by priests in their food, while the camel, which also was supposed to be unclean, was conveniently swallowed by them (Lev. 11:4). Such was the hypocrisy followed by the priests of the times of Jesus. Prophetic denouncement therefore, came heavily upon them.

One most notable point about the 'Prophetic Witness' in the biblical tradition is that prophets in general appeared whenever 'poor and needy' were oppressed and injustice got widespread. Here are few examples to support of this point. Prophet Isaiah addressed the Lord on behalf of the poor and needy, when they suffered:

> For you have been refused to the poor (*la-dal*), a refuse to the needy in their distress, a shelter from the rain-storm and a shade from the heat (Is. 25: 4).

Prophet Jeremiah brought the message of the Lord to rich royal family of King Josiah of Judah and reminded them by saying:

> He judged the cause of the poor and needy, then it was well. Is not this to know me? Says the Lord. But your eyes and heart are only on your dishonest gain, For shedding innocent blood, And for practicing oppression and violence (Jer. 22: 16-17).

Prophet Amos used much stronger language while addressing the people of Israel, as they had become oppressors of the needy and the poor and got corrupted in every sphere of their life. He said to them;

> Hear this, you trample on the needy,
> bring ruin to poor (*ani*) of the land,
> saying, "when the new moon be over
> so that we may sale grain;
> and the Sabbath, So that we may offer wheat for sale?
> We will make ephod small and the shekel great,
> and practice deceit with false balances,
> buying the poor (*dalim*) or silver,
> and needy for a pair of sandals,
> and selling the sweepings of wheat (Am. 8: 4-6)

The various oppressed groups were in the focus in mission manifesto that was revealed in the beginning of his ministry by Prophet of the prophets, Jesus Christ.

> The Spirit of the Lord is upon me,
> Because he has anointed me to bring good news to the poor.
> He has sent me to proclaim release to the captives,
> and recovery of right to the blind,
> to let the oppressed (*in Hindi translation 'Dalit'*) go free (Lk.4:18).

Besides such Biblical references against the exploitation and oppression of the poor and needy, the message of the entire Bible is also centered on two divine interventions pointing in the same direction. On the one hand the message affirms that God takes the side of oppressed, poor and the needy (Ex. 3: 7-12) and on the other, that God liberates the oppressed (Lk. 4:18-19). The second intervention, besides offering the liberation to the various oppressed groups of human beings (subaltern), also offers hope for their future by proclaiming "the year of the Lord's favour" (Lk. 4:19), which means that time of their liberation is coming. One most important factor in all the prophecies and proclamations of both the Old and the New Testaments (as pointed by Bishop Newbigus) is that these speak of liberation or salvation in terms of actual historical happenings, and not as "a matter of intellectual contemplation or mystical union; it is a matter of doing justice and mercy in concrete situations"[15] (Jer. 22:6; 1 John 4:8, Cf. 3: 14-24). An Indian theologian, Fr. L. Stanislaus, affirms this when he says, "Since the Gospel is linked to the concrete lives of the people, the Church's proclamation includes the issue of human rights, social justice, equality, peace, and development."[16] Bishop Julio Labayan of Philippines also sums up his discussion on 'prophetic mission' of the Church saying: "Here task and mission is simply to continue the history of salvation, that her founder, Jesus Christ, inaugurated and sealed with his blood...Here too lies the purpose and rationale of transforming the Church from the historical model of a Christendom (imperialist) Church to that of the Church of the poor. The purpose and rationale of the Church's mission is to be light, leaven and salt of the earth towards making the earth a place where God of love, justice and peace will be at home with His people and His whole creation".[17]

At the end of the discussion I would like to refer once again to Edinburgh 2010 Conference to see if any concrete direction can be sought from it that can contribute to our understanding of 'prophetic witness' in India. It may be too early to do this because all the Conference documents in the final form are not available yet. But some of the observations made by the nine study groups, which I had the chance to glance through, can be quite helpful. For example, the report of Group one on 'Foundations for Mission' says, "The popular understanding of mission...were proclamation expected to result in numerical Church groups and pastoral care. Similarly social justice and resistance to oppression were also recognized as God's mission. However, these two aspects of mission were not fully integrated.[18] The report of Group three on 'Mission and Post-modernists' points to the old adage: 'Witness! If necessary use words', and insists that this adage "needs pondering by all who want to share their faith. Christian service and issues of justice are integrated to the Gospel. A Church that forgets its prophetic role, struggling for peace and the integrity of creation and combating injustice, is not only losing its credibility, but betraying its calling."[19] The report of Group eight on 'Mission and Unity – Ecclesiology and Mission' goes still further and brings the four essential aspects of mission to the fore, while referring to 'reconciliation' as the new emerging paradigm of mission. Making a reference to Athens Report of 2005 which contains a statement on mission as reconciliation 'in the power of the Spirit' in the context of a broken world, the Group eight observes, "Truth, memory, justice and forgiveness are understood as essential aspects needed within both the Church and the society at large to enable the dynamic of the reconciliation and healing process."[20]

IV. Conclusion: the God-given Agenda for the Church

Based upon the discussion of this paper, an agenda can be drawn that would focus on the present needs in the Indian context and what is expected of the Church:

1. To remove caste discriminations from all sections of our people, particularly from Christians. This entails full restoration to the Dalits of their deprived rights, dignity and freedoms.

2. To give due recognition to the cultures of the Adivasis (Tribals) and grant them their demands that pertain to their identity, security and unhindered continuity related to their rights to water, land, forest and identity.

3. To reintroduce Justice in all spheres of human relationships and activities (the economic, the social, the political, the cultural and the religious), because the Divine Justice is implanted in all these rights.

4. To restore the inalienable Rights that every human is endowed with but which are denied (or suppressed or reduced) to many in this land. The State, the power structures, lack of consciousness, and other agencies need to be challenged to restore them.

5. To eliminate Gender discrimination in every walk of life, and, to begin with, in the Church. Gender complementarities and equality

are the Will of God and to flout them is defiance of the divine in and by the creatures of God.

6. To eliminate conflicts among Hindus, Muslim, Christians and other religious groups, and to strengthen the culture of dialogue and mutual interaction of a creative nature among religions, since these originate from God,

7. To deal with the problem of fundamentalism in religions and endeavour to forge alliances among religions to work for the realization of social goals. Such authentic engagement with the social agenda helps the original religious inspiration to be progressively re-interpreting itself, making it relevant to every age and situation.

8. To abolish child labour from our midst and to safeguard the future of our children. We have to create healthy atmosphere for them, especially the disadvantaged.

9. To abolish the existing economic disparity among the people, eliminate poverty and indigence, and strive for the all-round welfare of God's people.

10. To support and strengthen the efforts to safeguard the secular and democratic fabric of the society. The multi-ethnic and multi-religious composition of the nation demands respect for diversity as a value and eliciting collaboration from all.

11. To strive to heal the injuries and wounds of the past by the release of the power of Truth, and of forgiveness and reconciliation, based on Justice and Love.

God intervenes in history identifying Himself with those who suffer enslavement and oppression and liberates them. It is our task and privilege to collaborate with God in this task. We firmly hold that when we join the struggle of those who have been committed to secure their much awaited liberation we shall in fact be collaborating with God, and that will be our prophetic witness.

The Indian Church (which includes 'the Church of North India') therefore needs to respond to this challenge by committing herself to decisive action. If this opportunity to act is missed or allowed to pass by, the loss for the Church in India, for the Gospel, and for all the people of this nation will be immeasurable. Jesus wept over Jerusalem due to its people's inability to perceive their *Kairos*. Will the Indian Church be able to perceive her *Kairos* that is at hand? As far as the Church of North India is concerned she has done well in this direction up till now as we have seen in the story of the development of her mission concept; but now the time (*Kairos*) has come for her to go for all out action, based on a well-planned road map to implement the God-given agenda to us.

Endnotes

[1] Quotation in: *Ibid.*, p.2.

[2] CNI Synodical Programme "Towards a Holistic Understanding of Mission, a Report, New Delhi, 1993, p. 134.

[3] Gairdner, W.H.T. :"Edinburgh 1910" An Account and Interpretation of the world Mission Conference, Edinburgh, 1910, pp. 6,7.

[4] *Ibid.*, pp. 137,138.

[5] Unpublished Report on *'Theme One: Foundations for mission'* Edinburgh, 2010, p. 11.

[6] Unpublished Report on *'Theme Eight: Mission and Unity Ecclesiology and Mission'*, Edinburgh 2010, p. 214.

[7] *Plan of Church Union in North India and Pakistan.* Fourth Revised Edition. Madras, 1965, pp. 10, 11.

[8] *Churches' Role in Social Service and Development, Synodical Board of Social Service.* Church of North India. Consultation held in Calcutta. November 1978. New Delhi. 1989 (reprinted), p. 21.

[9] *Transfer of Vision.* A Leadership Development Programme Church of North India (LDP-CNI), 1984-86. Calcutta. 1984, p. 8.

[10] Minutes of the 9th Ordinary Meeting of the Synod of the Church of North India. S:9:95-542:C, p. 18.

[11] *Ibid.*, (S:9: 95-542:II-h), p. 22.

[12] Draft Minutes of the 11th Ordinary Synod of CM, held on 4th-8th. October, 2001. New Delhi. S:11: 01 — 677(1), p.22.

[13] *CNI Synodical Programme "Towards a Holistic Understanding of Mission"*, Consultation on "Church: A Community in Mission for Justice. Peace and

Integrity of Creation." 15-17 November. 1993. New Delhi, A Report. pp. x, xi.

[14] *Ibid.*, p. 134.

[15] Newbigin, Lessilie: *The Open Secret, An Introduction to the Theology of mission* (Revised Edition), SPCK, 1995, p.23.

[16] Stanislaus, L.: *The Liberative Mission of the Church Among Dalit Christian*, ISPCK, Delhi, 1999, p.291.

[17] Labayan, Julio: *op.cit.*, p.60.

[18] Unpublished Report on *'Theme One: Foundations for mission'* Edinburgh, 2010, p. 34.

[19] Unpublished Report on *'Theme Three: Mission and Postmodernities'* Edinburgh 2010, p. 78.

[20] Unpublished Report on *'Theme Eight: Mission and Unity Ecclesiology and Mission'*, Edinburgh 2010, p. 217.

Affirming Unity, Proclaiming Justice

Exploring a New Mission Agenda in a Fractured World

– S.R. Cutting

We greatly rejoice and celebrate completion of 40 years of our journey together in the Church of North India. The Church of North India was inaugurated on 29th November 1970 at Nagpur with the motto **"Unity Witness and Service"** written on its emblem.

Unity of the body of Christ

Jesus had envisioned that the body of all believers from different nationalities, cultures and languages would be bound together into one body some day. Hence he had prayed as recorded in John 17:20-21 "_____ **May they be one, so that the world will believe that you sent me."** He also proclaimed in John 10:16 – **"There are other sheep which belong to me that are not of this sheepfold _____ they will listen to my voice, and they will become one flock with one shepherd."**

The movement towards coming together of the fragmented body of Christ started in Edinburgh one hundred years ago through the historic Missionary Conference. We are also celebrating completion of a century of that Ecumenical movement which started in 1910 in Edinburgh. Church of South India was the first fruit in India of that Ecumenical movement which was inaugurated on 19th September 1947. The Church of North India became a tangible reality in the year 1970 on 29th November at Nagpur. This is the Lord's doing and is marvellous in our sight and understanding.

The ecumenical journey is continued and another important milestone was reached when conciliary union of Church of North India, Church of South India and Mar Thoma Church matured into formation of Communion of Churches in India. We praise God that we are moving under the guidance of His Spirit, towards wider union of Churches in India.

'Ecumenism' is a word that has been derived from "Oikumene", a Greek adjective meaning the whole inhabited earth. Therefore, we must always keep in mind that the unity of Churches is at the service of the unity of the whole humankind of which Churches are servants. Further more, the human race is entrusted with the stewardship of all creation, so that the "integrity of creation" falls within the ultimate scope of ecumenism. The Church is uniting to bring together the divided and broken human kind to work for the complete redemption of the 'Oikumene'.

Proclaiming Justice

The word 'Justice' is described by the Oxford dictionary as – (Just behaviour or treatment; the quality of being fair and reasonable; the administration of law in a fair and reasonable way). Because God is holy and righteous, He demands justice be practised among human being in all their dealings, especially while dealing with the vulnerable, the poor, orphans, widows and the under privileged. See Leviticus 19:15 and Ps.82:3, Isaiah 56:1, Amos 5:24 – **"Let justice roll down like waters, and righteousness like an ever flowing stream." "Give justice to the weak and the orphan; maintain the right of the lowly and the**

destitute. Rescue the weak and the needy; deliver them from the hands of the wicked." (Psalm 82:3-4).

India is a very fast developing economy. Everyone is excited about the rate of growth of our economy which is around 8 to 8.5% per annum. Because of heavy Foreign Direct Investment (F.D.I.) in Indian Companies, strong growth of I.T. sector and other industries and even the agriculture sector showing slow but steady growth, the economic growth was sustained even when the world was passing through economic depression. The benefits of this growth however are limited to about 30% of India's Population, a large majority of our people are bereft of any benefits. They are poor, resource less, lack education, health care and capital. Therefore, there are struggles by the people for justice, human rights and human dignity at different levels. The struggles are against disparities between the rich and the poor, which find expressions in Naxalite and Maoist movements, increasing crimes of loot and thefts etc. Evils of exploitations and injustices abound because of the large number of vulnerable people. Adivasis, Harijans, Scheduled Castes, landless peasants, urban workers, fishermen, rickshaw pullers etc. are aware today more than ever before, and are crying for justice.

The Church of North India believes in Jesus' Nazareth Manifesto (Luke 4:16-18) as the declaration of Jesus' mission on earth. Therefore, the Church's mission is the same as Jesus' mission because Jesus is the Head of the Church and the Church is his Body carrying on His mission on earth. Proclaiming justice as an essential part of the mission is part of Nazareth manifesto. So the Church gets involved in the struggles of the people for justice.

Towards a New Mission Agenda

The motto of CNI is Unity, Witness and Service. Her mission statement states "**The Church of North India as a United and Uniting together is committed to announce the Good News of the reign of God inaugurated through death and resurrection of Jesus Christ in** proclamation and to demonstrate in actions to restore the integrity of God's Creation through continuous struggle against the demonic powers by breaking down the barriers of caste, class, gender, economic inequality and exploitation of the nature."

The new mission agenda, within the scope of the CNI Mission Statement could include the following:

1. *Proclamation of the Gospel*

Because the new covenant offered by Jesus Christ is for all, it must be proclaimed to all as the greatest good news through various Conventional and unconventional methods. The benefits of Jesus' incarnation and sacrificial offering of his life must be not only proclaimed but also explained to all who would listen and open up their hearts to the new covenant. Always be mindful that we live in the midst of religious pluralism, growing disharmony within the society due to religious fundamentalism and communal tensions. How to strike a balance between Ecumenism and Evangelism must be a part of special training for all Presbyters, Deacons and Evangelists especially and also laity in general. Richard Stoll Armstrong writing an article for the Westminster's Dictionary of Christian Theology says – (pp.193):

> "The challenge to the contemporary Church is how to do evangelism in a pluralistic world, how to be both ecumenical and evangelical at the same time, affirming the truth of other faiths without compromising the uniqueness of Christ …….. Evangelism will have integrity when it is done by Christian congregations who understand themselves as servant people of God, called first to seek kingdom of God and his righteousness and to follow where the Lord of the Church leads them."

It would be worthwhile to consider in how many ways we use our gifts of the Holy Spirit for evangelization. Some fundamentalist in our country are opposing the spread of the Gospel, spreading false propaganda about Christian missionary activity. We must not respond with Christian fundamentalism but with greater commitment to Holy Spirit's Work in and through our life. We must use all our opportunities to communicate Christ where ever we are placed by God.

2. To Teach, Baptise and Nurture New Believers

It has been observed that Christian values are gradually vanishing from the life of Christian families and individuals. Many Christian parents are not inculcating Christian values in their children. They do not even encourage their children to go to Sunday Schools, Confirmation classes, Vacation Bible Schools, Youth Bible Study and Prayer groups, Schools/ Colleges offering Bible and moral classes or to mission workshops and seminars. The obvious consequences of such up bringing, bereft of Christian values is that as a community we are loosing our impact upon the wider society as the salt of the earth/light of the world (Matthew 5:13-16) or as leaven of the earth (Matthew 13:33). It is of utmost importance that provisions should be seriously made for Christian nurture of Children, young adults and even senior adults so that Christian witness and service offered by the Christian Community would become powerful means of mission involvement.

For the new believers, both young and old, regular teaching and practical training of Christian faith must be ensured at Pastorate level and if possible at Diocesan level. Such teaching is essential before baptism is administered and it must be continued after baptism till Confirmation of the new believers. At many places new Churches are being planted. Many new believers are coming to Christ. They need regular Christian nurture and up building of Christian character. Often there are issues of social and economic boycott to be dealt with by the new believers. There are caste restrictions in India which are carried over to the Church by the new believers and many old believers also suffer from caste considerations within the Church.

How can the Church deal with the entire above very complex and challenging issues? The new mission agenda must be based on promptings of God the Holy Spirit. The Church must wait upon the Lord and spend time in prayer and meditation before deliberating upon, suggesting and planning new mission paradigms. What is at stake for the Church in India? The very **"Unity, Witness and Service"** it proclaims as its motto, is at stake if our new and old believers deny the motto of the Church by a life – style contradictory to the declared motto. Therefore, nurture of all believers, young and old is of utmost importance.

3. *To Respond to Human Needs by Loving Service*

Jesus' mandate to his disciples was that they should serve others just as he himself came to the world to serve and lay down his life as a ransom for many – Matthew 20:26-28, Mark 9:35 and 10:43-45, Luke 22:25-27, John 13:12-15 and Philippians 2:5-8.

The Church in India has been serving the society at large for about three hundred years through services rendered in the crucial areas of 'Education' 'Health Care' and 'Socio-economic' development of the most deprived and marginalized sections of our Society. Church has been largely responsible to educate, conscientise and awaken the Dalits, tribals, people of backward classes and marginal farmers and labourers. Even the people of higher castes have been greatly benefited from services offered by the Church. The contributions of the Church in all the above areas have been recognized and are still proclaimed and highly respected.

In 21st Century, India is a fast developing country. The cost of fast pace of economic development has to be borne by a large majority of people who may or may not benefit in any way, by the development all around. The cost may include loosing one's profession, because one's skills become redundant. New skills and technology has to be accepted and adopted. New avenues of service sector of the nation make it necessary to acquire new skills. Large number of people becomes unemployable while job opportunities are mushrooming. This creates a lot of discontentment, strife, envy and also crime increases. Agriculture is progressively becoming less profitable as the cost of inputs is going up every year. To top it all, communalism, religious fundamentalism, and corruption in public life are factors that are creating rifts, enmity, hatred and unrest. All of this is making India a very fractured/divided society. The rest of the world is also fractured because of terrorism, wars, economic imbalances and social revolutions in Africa and parts of Asia.

The Church is an instrument of God's mission in the world and it has been called to serve the society to offer/administer the New Covenant to all. Jesus said, **"Peace be with you! As the Father has sent me, I am sending you...."** John 21:21. The new covenant, sealed by the blood of Jesus Christ offers a paradigm of love, care, sacrificial living and responding to human need by loving service. Services in the areas of education, health care and socio-economic development should be continued with full commitment and zeal. More emphasis should be laid on professional education in our Schools and Colleges. New Schools and Colleges, especially for professional training should be opened to cater to the crying need of developing and honing new skills in order to produce employable human resource.

The Good Samaritan model of services rendered during natural disasters, e.g. Tsunamis, earthquakes, floods, draughts etc. must be continued and further strengthened. It could be very useful to generate and maintain emergency Funds at Synod level, Diocesan level even Pastorate level as also to train human resource willing to render services during natural disasters, epidemics, rail/road accidents etc.

4.   *To Seek to Transform Unjust Structures of Society*
Churches in India have been blessed with national level structures such as – National Council of Churches, Communion of Churches in India, All India Christian Council Catholic Bishops' Conference of India and several other regional level organisations. But how many national or regional level people's movements have we witnessed? Can we name a few movements under the guidance and empowerment of God the Holy Spirit?

We can only think of agitations by Christians against Freedom of Religion bill and recently the Dalit Christian Movement for reservations in Government jobs. Against persecution of Christians only not Muslim or Sikhs, there have been some agitations. Does this dismal record of Church in India point to a basic lack of interest in the involvement in urgent national issues, international issues and regional issues? God forbid that the SALT of the earth, the LIGHT of the World and the LEAVEN of the society be interested in its own welfare and security only (Matthew 5:13-16 and 13:33).

"Ecumenical missiology opts to envision a society where the social evils suffered by various sectors of people shall be eradicated. It has a prophetic vision of liberation of all captives of human traditions and socio-cultural institutions." (Dr. Siga Arles for an article "Prophetic vision in contemporary Missiologies." Printed by ISPCK–'Mission Paradigm in the New Millennium' Pages 130).

Ecumenical missiology is based on Church's active role in dealing with issues of justice, peace, integrity of creation, national harmony, development and social change. The Church has a prophetic vision to bring down the structures of injustice and seek to establish just patterns, to fight corruption in public life, to seek to eradicate poverty by striking at the root causes of poverty, to break every form of slavery and liberate people into abundant life which Jesus Christ is establishing in new humanity.

All this may sound very presumptuous on the part of the Church to take up as its mission, because of the lack of resources, both human resource and other resources. But we must remember that Church is the new humanity Jesus Christ has created to work on earth under the guidance and strength of God the Holy Spirit. Church prays every day in the words of its Lord – **"Thy kingdom come, thy will be done on earth as it is in heaven,"** and works very hard to fulfil the prayer with full commitment.

5. *To Strive to Safeguard the Integrity of Creation and Renew the Life of the Earth*

The stewardship of God's creation was given to humankind to have full control over all created beings. When stewards are given absolute powers, they are called to more responsibility and accountability. We see in Genesis 1:28-30 and 2: 8-9, 15-20 – "... **Be fruitful and multiply and fill the earth and subdue it and have dominion over the fish of the sea and the birds of heaven and over every living thing that moves on the earth .... I have given you every plant yielding seed .... You shall have them for food ..... to every beast ..... every bird ..... every thing that creeps on earth ..... I have given every green plant for food ..... The Lord God planted a garden in Eden .... there he put**

the man he had created ….. He put him in the garden of Eden to work it and keep it …."

The words sound like God giving charge to humankind for all He had created and explaining the purposes for which they were created. Putting humankind in the Garden of Eden to work and keep and protect it was symbolic for his total responsibility of the planet earth. The kind of stewardship humankind would exercise; it would be responsible for the welfare of fauna and flora, the earth/soil, the atmospheric balance, temperature and pressure. The marine life and total ecological balance of the earth has to be maintained in order that life be maintained and continuously renewed. A steward is manager. The manager's task is to serve the interests of the owner. Christian stewardship is the management of all our resources on behalf of God.

In an article written for 'Mission Paradigm in the new Millennium,' Dr. J. Patmury observes (p. 366) – "Not only does God view all creation as good, but God shows intimate relation with it. God's first blessing recorded in the Genesis story, is for the fish and the birds. God blessed them saying, be fruitful and multiply and fill the waters in the sea, and let birds multiply on the earth. (Gen. 1:22). And Jesus would say: look at the birds of the air, they neither sow nor reap, nor gather into barns, and yet your heavenly Father feeds them – (Matthew 6:26). If God cares for and nurtures them, then as God's stewards humans are to do the same."

We need to ask questions about Church's stewardship reflected in its programmes. There is a great awakening all around us about global warming and its ill effects threatening the very existence of life on the planet. The Church is called to provide a model of perfect stewardship of God's creation, and lead all other people towards responsible stewardship.

Conclusion

The Church of North India is 40 years old but its proclamation of Unity within the body of Christ is yet to be fully realized. The Church is partially united seeking full unity and oneness of mission agenda, albeit with diverse and multifacious missional programmes.

The Church often discusses its mission statement, mission programmes, seeks to evolve new mission paradigms at mission Conferences and workshops, but the ground reality is that most of its members are not truly interested in missional involvement. Some are interested in their own welfare and benefits accruing to them as members because they are from Dalit or tribal background, educationally, socially and economically background. Many are interested in Dalit Christian movement asking for reservations in Govt: jobs. Some are frighten because of well planned persecution of Christians, especially in areas where evangelism and Church planting ministries are being carried out. Therefore, we need to start with evangelism, teaching and nurture of our own people. Express unity in concrete terms when persecution breaks out and prepare them for missional programmes as per the Church's mandate/commission given by the Lord. (Matt: 28:19-20, John 21:21).

There are programmes the Church is carrying on in the areas of social justice, restoration of human rights, and grassroots level implementation of Government programmes for the B.P.L. B.C. and O.B.C. people. The participation of Churches in these ministries should be greatly enhanced. Church's participation in the ministry of education and health care must be enhanced. New avenues of such services are to be explored.

May God, the Holy Spirit, continue to enlighten and empower the Church to fulfil its Commission on earth.

Affirming Unity, Proclaiming Justice

Exploring a New Mission Agenda in a Fractured World

– Sadhona Ganguli

L et us today reflect on the truth, *"We must never forget that God's intervention is to overcome chaos and restore the order that was established during creation."*

When we read the Declaration of the United Nations Millennium Goals, it directs our attention to the collective human responsibility "to uphold the principles of human dignity, equality and equity and our duty especially to the **most vulnerable** and in particular, the children of the world to whom the future belongs, to the World commitment, to deal with global poverty in all its forms by 2015. "

The CNI Vision

The struggle of People for achieving human dignity and justice is the vision of the ministry of the Church as envisaged in the plan of union of the CNI. Yet as a Movement we realize that we have not fully utilized our united strength to realize measurable goals. Each Church/ Congregation has its own experience of spirituality and social outreach. However, we have not been able to tap the huge potential for united action.

In the context of the United Nations Millennium Goals and the reality of a fractured world, where thoughtless humanity continues to ravage and marginalise Nature, Dalits and Women, we as Churches and individual Christians, together with the whole CNI Movement, as it celebrates 40 years of its ecumenical journey this year, are challenged to examine our life and actions and radically change ourselves as a Movement.

1. *Key Players*

The CNI in the light of the Biblical perspective on Liberation and the image of Women and Men, being made in the "image of God, having an inter-relationship, bearing joint responsibility for Nurturing, Recreating and transforming Nature and Society, through the "Good News," should focus more urgently on releasing the potential of women – who are the key players in families and community life and thus enable them in partnership with men to break the shackles of oppression and poverty in every community. This will have a multiplied effect in achieving all millennium goals.

Women through the ages have been equally used, by God to bring His salvation and redeeming Grace to the suffering people. In the Old Testament, we find several examples (Esther; Ruth; Miriam Ex.2:1-10; 15:1-22; Ruth 1:15-17) and many others. The New Testament lists women as bearers of "New Life". Jesus values each person Women are equally valuable as men be it to be given insights or becoming bearers of the Gospel message or being builders of the early church. The Samaritan Woman (to whom Jesus explains the meaning of "Living water" and of "True Worship", Dorcas, raised from the dead by Peter goes on to be a faithful disciple; Lydia, the business woman who gave all her support to the early disciples; Mary Magdalene, was chosen to receive and convey the first news of the Resurrection (References: Jn.4:7-27; Rom.12:2-5; Mk.10:45; Cor.12:12). In respect to all these examples noted here we have to find out that from where have we inculcated the thought that women are not equal or competent or fit to serve God or to humanity as capably as men? Perhaps, it begins with the kind of family structures, attitudes and practices that we find in our Churches and communities.

2. The Commitment

Committed, as a body of Christian Disciples, to proclaim Jesus' Message of Liberation (Luke 4: 14-21) and the ministry which God has entrusted to us and reflected in the passage which Jesus read out from Isaiah 61:1-2, that we His people have to be co-workers with Him for the fulfillment of his commandments in our times: He has anointed me to,

1. to preach the Gospel to the poor

2. heal the brokenhearted

3. preach deliverance to the captives

4. recover the sight to the blind

5. set at liberty the oppressed

6. proclaim the year of the Lord

3. Transformation: What is Jesus' message to us about Transforming Inequalities in Family life?

Let us learn from a seemingly shocking statement of Jesus about Family Life, "I have come to set a man against his Father, a daughter against her Mother, and a daughter-in law against her Mother-in-law(Math.10:34-37). In these three relationships the powerful exploits the weak. In the present days we find this word coming true as we find this truth existing in our Society particularly, true in respect to women. When we study the role and position of women in different spheres of decision making: Health, Education, Employment, Life style, we observe that the range of options taken by women are shaped by the decisions made within a family and these in turn are influenced by the socialization process. Most decisions are influenced by Structures and Patriarchal values deeply engraved within families and the society. These decisions are mostly oppressive towards women and they lower the self esteem and confidence of women more importantly her potential to be a "change maker" in the family, Church and Society. A thorough change is needed in our Society as well as in the Families so that, everyone gets an equal opportunity to grow and become complete human beings—to be able to serve the Church and Society completely encouraging the active role of Ordained women in the Ministry.

4. *Building up a Christ-Centered Value Base*

The CNI movement needs to concentrate on building up a Christ centered base of Values, Knowledge and skills, to transform Attitudes and Practices within Christian families and congregations.

Knowledge

To have the thorough knowledge of Facts, and Information that will enable the decision making and access to life and career options.

Skills

To develop skills in Communication, Assertiveness, Relationship building, Conflict Resolution and Negotiating—all these provide the means for effective use of Knowledge. Capacity building in the art of "speaking the Truth with love" within families/Congregation life/ Civic and Social life is essential.

Attitudes

To develop insights and tools for Self Understanding through Value Education, Clarifying doubts and Counseling for further enhancement of our skills, especially those leading to the decisions and setting priorities. These factors are inter -related and they influence each other and our social and Congregational life.

Each one of us needs to examine his/ her values that shape our attitudes, actions and practices. What is their origin? Where do they come from? i) Father ii) Mother iii) Relatives iv) Teachers v) Friends; vi) Religion; vi) Customs; vii) Others.

Which are the values that are important to a person? How did they/ one of them get demonstrated in his or her life? What happened at Church or Theological College or during the arrangements for a marriage in the family? What did go against his or her Christian values that made him or her cringe with shame at the indignity on someone through an "ostentatious" marriage or a dowry demand in consideration of marriage? It could be about treatment of a child domestic worker at home? In such situations Is it possible that someone can take a strong stand against the tide of negative decision making that is against Christ values and also against Human Rights?

5. *Working within Gods Plan: for healing and restoration of Women and Nature by Expanding our Knowledge Base*

We must open our eyes, hearts and minds and to look through the eyes of Jesus at the world round us with all the inequalities and injustice, to the imbalances we have brought into Nature through our greedy lifestyles we need to open our eyes, our hearts and our minds to realize the harsh realities in our world today. Let us learn to react and respond when Headlines scream from Newspapers and Journals .

And the violence continues:

*   **Rape**: There is no Age no bar of the Rape victim, No Caste bar. We have witnessed cases of rape occurring to girl child right from infants to Toddlers to middle aged to even Grandmothers. All age categories have shown to have been raped (within families and in public spheres).

*   **Violence against Women:** *"In India, every 26 minutes a woman is molested. Every 34 minutes a woman is raped. Every 42 minutes a woman is sexually harassed .Every 43 minutes a woman is kidnapped. Every 93 minutes a woman is killed. And those are just the cases which are reported. (Source: AASRA)*

*   **Dowry Deaths/Harassment**: *"Young housewife burnt alive for dowry"*; *"woman's Body found floating" " Life ends due to Dowry harassment"*; *"young married commits suicide, unable to adjust"*

*   **Female Foeticide** and discrimination of girl children: The growing gender imbalance in India is scandalous. We must strongly campaign against the unethical and illegal practices of using the Pre-natal diagnostic tests to discover the sex of the child and to abort girl children. We need to inculcate positive attitude in families about both the girl and boy children. We need to develop Vigilance against commercial medical diagnostics promoting sex selection

and such agencies should be black listed be it medical practitioners or families, going in for such tests. We as the followers of Christ have a committed duty to change the mindset of people which has been affects the statistics that shows growing gender imbalance in recent years in our country.

• **Social exclusion**: This is another cruel way by which certain sections of society are disadvantaged and excluded on the basis of: Caste, Religion, Gender, Descent, Color, Disability, Health Status-HIV status and so on. Discrimination occurs everywhere, from the wider fields of Legal, Educational Professional or Health services, to the confines of families, homes and the social life even in the hierarchy and language of Church life.

6. *Changing Attitudes*

The CNI has been in the vanguard of the Ecumenical movement in opening up its portals to Leadership for theologically trained and Women Lay leaders. Yet, Alas! We have never heard anywhere about a church member saying that in the conclusion of a Funeral service conducted by a woman Presbyter "I wish this service was done by the male "Padresaab" it would have been proper and blessed."?

Feminist Theology is taught in Theological colleges but what are we doing to make Church postings of women Presbyters more gender friendly? What efforts are we making to encourage congregations to respect Women Presbyters.? Or are we encouraging more talented and spiritually inclined women to opt for theological studies and a life of service to the Church? Are we working towards creation of a cadre of trained women and men for leadership within both the Clergy as well as Laity? Are we trying to develop true partnership of women and men for transformation of Congregational life and the Churches in India?

After recognizing these realities expressed in either ways within our societies we need to urgently plan to transform ourselves, the ways and thoughts of people in such a way to bring solidarity among women and develop an attitude of real partnership of women and men: to "build Communities of Justice and Peace" in our Family lives and our

Homes, Our Educational Systems, Our Employment Practices ensuring Protection for the handicapped, abused and exploited through change in our life styles, attitudes and values; to transform the Church, Nation and Society at large.

7.   *The Journey forward, in Faith:*

As the CNI's journey continues ahead it needs to focus on cruel social realities within the context of which its member churches and congregations are functioning particularly, in the majority of rural, tribal and Dalit Christian communities. The movement for Justice and protection of Human rights in the secular world challenges us to realize our strength as a united Christian movement to work more creatively, for the well- being of the poor oppressed and marginalized.

The institutions of Education and Healthcare within the CNI network must become the centers for transforming the lives of the poor. All we have to do is work creatively, in Faith, to fulfill God's mission through our lives .Every congregation must become a 'Serving Congregation' free of its social separations and exclusions. Every congregation should have a strong partnership of men and women to nurture spiritual growth and positive values within its membership of families.

As part of its core plan for the next decade, the Church of North India needs to focus on major Perspective building workshops across congregations to create a true Disciples of Christ that are seeking to serve and witness through Fellowship and sacrificial lifestyles. This must be planned and channelised through, organized units like, Sunday Schools, Youth Fellowships, Women's Fellowships and Social service-outreach programmes, with a definite aim of enabling people to break free of false patriarchal values that are responsible factors for sustained Inequalities and Injustice in Churches and society at large.

This Process must address:

1.   Key Players

2.   The Commitment

3. Issues of Inequalities in Family life?

4. Building up a Christ centered Value base in congregations and families

5. Gods plan, for healing and restoration of Women and Nature by expanding our Knowledge base

6. Bringing about attitudinal change

7. Developing deeper spiritual strengths in the Laity

To conclude in the words of Dr K. C. Abraham *"Ministry is broader than administering the sacraments and preaching the Word of God. It is what the people together do and how they live out their Faith. In this sense it is a community endeavour"*.

Then, Let us all be united and thank God for His many mercies on the Church of North India for the last forty years and move forward into the future, in Faith, with new perspectives, for the fulfillment of God's mission in India today.

Healing a Broken World: Pastoral Perspectives on Missiological Praxis

Relevant Mission Engagements to Transform Broken Communities

– Philip Jadhav

The word 'mission', till very recent time in India, was considered as an exclusive expression of 'Christian' activity associated with the 'missionaries'. And such 'mission' work was viewed as engagements undertaken by the 'foreigners' representing overseas mission boards. The nature and purpose of such mission work undertaken by foreign missionaries was generally viewed with suspicion since it was supposed to 'influence' religious beliefs of the local people in promoting Christianity. The mission activity during the colonial rule in India was generally perceived as beneficiary of the largesse extended by imperial patronage and closely associated with the foreign rulers.

However, In India of today, the understanding of the word 'mission' has undergone dramatic change, particularly post globalization, liberalization and opening up of the Indian market. Today, titles of several flagship programmes of the government of India in the field of health, education and development include the word 'mission' to denote focused initiatives undertaken with 'missionary' zeal to transform and improve social and economic conditions of the disadvantaged people.

Historical Missionary Engagements: Impact on Social Realities

The historical missionary engagements in the field of health, education, agriculture etc. in India, inspired by Christian mission commitment to serve the poor, needy and weak, coincided with the advent of the colonial rule in the country. The nature and form of mission work generally involved imparting of educational instructions and training to equip the local people with basic general knowledge, written and spoken language ability, vocational skills for livelihood etc., by starting educational, vocational and healthcare institutions. These faith based missionary efforts, genuinely committed to the Christian cause, however, did not impact the governance and administrative mechanism or the social systems and structures in the country responsible for exploitation and marginalisation of common people. The programmes, resources, planned and executed by missionaries with support of rulers for the upliftment of poor and disadvantaged had elements of charity and were devoid of any strategy essential for social transformation and change. The poor were thus seen to be the object of service and charity.

Though proclamation of Gospel was the primary objective of mission work, missionaries did attempt to introduce liberal western ideas and thought, in a limited manner, to encourage emancipation of people from regressive as well as repressive social traditions and dogmas. However, a kind of tacit status quo and neutrality was maintained in matters of political and economic exploitation and oppression of people by feudal rulers and the colonial power.

Rational for Mission Action: Relevance of Contextual Reality

Understanding of the mission tasks, as engagement of followers of Jesus Christ, committed to the agenda of resisting injustices and working for building equitable and harmonious communities, has to have a context. The contextual realities of people provide the reference for interpreting and understanding the message of the Bible and the will of God. The life, witness and ministry of Jesus Christ was rooted in the historical situations prevalent in Galilee and Jerusalem, and Jesus Christ was moved to act and change the circumstances responsible for the afflictions of the people.

Leading church historians and theologians have acknowledged and affirmed the fact that the form in which Jesus Christ, churches and Christian institutions were introduced and brought to India by European Christian missionaries was as per their Biblical perceptions and understanding based on their respective European circumstances, situations and historical experiences.

Many decades ago, D. T. Niles, a well-known Sri Lankan Church statesman, had said that Jesus Christ was brought to Asia as a potted plant. He further elaborated and said that just as the plant planted into the soil along with the pot surrounding it could not gather roots into the soil and blossom, the Gospel of Jesus Christ and church institutions brought to Asia in European forms, expressions, denominational affiliations, organizational structures, mission practices etc. could not effectively relate to the situations of local people who had distinct cultural and ethnic identities.

D. T. Niles went on to explain that the plant could gather roots in the soil and blossom only after the pot surrounding it was broken. It was therefore understood and recognized that the Biblical foundations for mission action has to be rooted in the local context, and read and interpreted from the perspective of people and communities living and experiencing unique circumstances and situations.

Historical Imperatives for Christian Unity and Witness

The evolution of church union in north India 40 years ago was prompted not only by the historical concern of the church regarding unity and witness of the Gospel but by a strong desire and conviction of church leaders and members to make the Christian faith relevant to the life situations of people including their social and cultural identities. Accordingly the united and uniting Church of North India came into being on 29th Nov 1970 to evolve and adopt unique identity and forms of worship, witness, and mission practices to reflect and relate the cultural diversity, hopes and aspirations of people of north India. The followers of Jesus Christ in India were convinced of the fact that the good news of liberating and healing the lives of the poor, captives and oppressed not only involves spiritual strengthening but also practical engagements to physically transform the exploitative social systems and structures responsible for incapacitating the people.

Theological Perspectives for Mission Action

The theological perspectives evolved, affirmed and adopted for Christian mission action and practices by CNI during the course of these 40 years has strived to focus on the contextual imperatives for Christian faith. The policy making structures of CNI Synod, Boards and Commissions, therefore, periodically interpreted the life and ministry of Jesus Christ in relation to the contemporary situation prevalent in the country, and underscored the ecumenical and inclusive dimension of Christian faith to work, act and restore dignity and respect to broken people. The members and congregations of CNI have thus been challenged from time to time to address critical social concerns impacting the communities within the respective geographical area towards fulfilling the Christian mission mandate of the church.

Important consultations of CNI on 'Churches' Role in Social Service and Development', 'Towards a Holistic Understanding of Mission' and CREEM prioritized mission concerns of justice and peace to build equitable and humane communities considering the quality of life experienced by majority of people in the country. However, in spite of fervent call for concerted mission action, the plight of urban poor in slums and shanty towns, and rural masses in inaccessible hinterlands across vast stretches of India, including large number of the church memberships, continue to be beset with unimaginable miseries. Sufferings are of exasperating proportions due to their inability to access education, health care, employment and means of livelihood essential for dignified living with respect.

Search for Alternate Mission Practices

The intention and purpose of forming the united CNI was to draw on the best traditions among the prevailing practices of the uniting churches to create contemporary and contextually relevant forms of Christian witness. However, in spite of good intentions and serious efforts during the 40 year life span, CNI has acknowledged the limitations within the organisation framework and has further resolved to the strengthen efforts required for evolving alternate models. The uniting church has to re-capture the intended spirit of unity and build on the platform created to bring together the rich material and experiential resources to relevantly witness the Gospel of Jesus Christ. The church has to develop much required new expressions, forms and tools to witness and practice Christian mission and affect transformation and social change to empower the dispossessed and incapacitated masses in the country.

Contemporary Social Realities: Exploitation of Natural Resources and Marginalisation of People

Status of Indian Parliamentary Democracy

Post independence, India adopted parliamentary form of democracy and government to initiate the process of nation building. The framework for democratic governance of the nation state assured every Indian citizen of the right to participate and contribute towards inclusive developmental efforts which would ensure progress, prosperity and well-being of all citizens. Unfortunately, the fundamental principles enshrined in the Constitution of the sovereign, socialist, secular, democratic Republic of India have been compromised very often by the divisive vote-bank party politics.

Shining India?

Among the community of nation states, India is generally projected as an economic power with a large, skilled work force specialising in information technology and financial services. Increased industrial production, growth in trade, commerce and foreign exchange reserves, enhanced nuclear capacity, and spectacular achievements in the field of space technology, has generally created an impression of all round prosperity in the country. However, the fact is that while there are a few who are counted among the richest in the world, about 80% of

Indian population lives in appalling poverty, earning less than half a US dollar or ₹25 per day. Alongside gleaming IT hubs in metropolitan cities, lives the largest slum population in the world without electricity, running water and sanitation, in the midst of unimaginable filth. More than 100,000 farmers have committed suicide during the last 10 years. India ranks lower than many countries of Sub Saharan Africa in the Human Development Index.

Liberalisation, Privatisation and Globalisation

India adopted the World Bank and International Monitoring Fund sponsored Structural Adjustment Programme for instituting economic reforms in the year 1991 resulting in the fundamental shift in the development strategy - replacement of an import – substitutive industrialization strategy by an export – oriented industrialization.

It was argued that the market-led growth model of liberalized economy, driven by the private sectors and foreign investment would generate higher growth rate and the efforts of this would trickle down to the poor masses in the country. The GDP growth increased substantially from 3-4% to reach 9% in the year 2007-08. Since then, the number of dollar millionaires increased manifold, as did the average income of top 10% of the population. However, the number of persons living in acute poverty during the same period continued to grow at alarming proportions.

Exploitation of Natural Resources for Growth Oriented Development

The growth oriented development model, riding high on increased production capacity by exploiting the natural resources, has had disastrous consequences for the people and the environment. The acquisition of traditional lands of farmers and tribals for commercial cropping, expressways and communication networks, mining, residential townships, transport hubs and Special Economic Zones for industrial projects etc. has displaced and dispossessed several lakhs of people in the different parts of the country. Similarly, to meet the demand for electricity to fuel the industrial production, dams have been built across several rivers to generate hydroelectric power, submerging several hundred thriving villages along with their histories and heritage. Damming and diversion of rivers has severely disrupted the downstream flows affecting sustenance, livelihoods and prosperity of lakhs of people along the river courses across the country.

Environmental Degradation and Displacement of People

The loss of traditional livelihood has forced people to migrate to metropolitan towns and cities, putting under pressure the inadequate infrastructure and services, and adding to the woes of urban chaos. Lack of employable vocational skills has forced migrants to survive by taking up menial jobs in unorganized sector, and find shelter in slums sacrificing their freedom and self respects.

Exploitation of land and water resources, particularly for heavy industrial projects, mining in forests and hills, and damming of rivers, has seriously impacted the environment and ecological balance, resulting in climate change and global warming.

Resistance Movements and Violation of Civil Liberties

The destitution and marginalisation of vast populations, in rural and tribal inhabited mineral rich areas, has magnified the rich/poor divide in the country, and the apathy of policy makers to their plight, has forced the peasants, farmers and tribals to organise themselves to protect and control their habitat. In several such resistance movements, the protestors against the anti-people development policies of the government, has resorted to armed struggle. Unable to control the anger and protests of the aggrieved populations, the governments have labeled the discontent and dissatisfaction of people, and their agitations to secure fundamental right to life and liberty, as per the article 21 of the Constitution, as insurgency and waging of war against the state.

To curb the growing uprising of the people, the state governments have not only unleashed the might of police and paramilitary forces, but have also invoked the anti-people legislations, as the Unlawful Activities Prevention Act (UAPA) and Armed Forces Special Powers Act, on the ground of "state security". Under the pretext of perceived threats to the state, several human rights activists have been detained and imprisoned, undermining the civil liberties and fundamental rights of the people.

Holistic and Contextually Relevant Mission Practices

The historical establishment and organization of the Church as the body of believers, and followers of Jesus Christ with a mission to proclaim the good news, involved not only preaching and teaching but also witnessing through service and action. The narratives in the Gospels, highlighting the life, witness and ministry of Jesus Christ, provide innumerable instances wherein He not only explained and taught about the Kingdom of God, but also demonstrated in action and practice, the process of building humane and equitable community, based on the Kingdom values of common good. The ministry of the church, to promote and practice the good news proclaimed by Jesus Christ, therefore has to be understood as an integrated responsibility of proclamation, evangelism and mission action for affecting social change.

Mission to Reconcile and Heal Brokenness

The indiscriminate exploitation of natural resources, and marginalisation of people, is a challenge to all believers commissioned to proclaim the good news, and participate in God's mission to uphold life, reconcile relationships, and restore peace and harmony for the well-being of everyone, everywhere. The destruction of life and environment all around us is also a reminder to the church that as primarily a community of worshippers to celebrate Eucharist and seek inspiration from Bible, work of building the kingdom of God also demands periodic renewal of creation. Working for promotion and practice of the kingdom values of justice and peace therefore involves the mission task and responsibility of engaging in sustainable development and ecological conservation.

A new creation and a new society is envisioned to manifest the characteristics of Jesus Christ by practicing reconciliation, restoring equitable relationships and preservation activities amidst the social struggles for justice, peace and alternative socio-economic system for sustainable development.

Mission to Liberate and Transform

Understanding mission as liberation is gaining momentum. The experience of faith based communities in Latin America to resist injustice and build humane and equitable society has enlarged understanding of Jesus Christ as redeemer from the tyranny of oppressive structures and systems.

The social realities experienced by people today are direct consequences of unjust and exploitative social and economic systems. To evolve pro-life and pro-people governance systems and structures, all people of God, the church, has to be mobilized to join the movement to stop destructive forces and encourage, support and strengthen initiatives working on alternatives models of development.

Enabling Organizational Structures for Mission

There is an urgent need for all of us to introspect, and acknowledge limitations within, to enable review and repositioning of organizational framework of the church. To begin with, the hierarchical model undermines the historical tradition and affirmation of the church bestowing priesthood to all believers. Equality in participatory decision making processes to evolve a plan of action for relevant mission engagement is very basic and central to the distinct characteristic of a faith community.

Study and Preparation to Participate in Mission

Bible is the primary source of information and inspiration to seek insights and knowledge about the will of God, kingdom of God, mission of God, Son of God, discipleship and responsibility entrusted for proclamation of the good news. To be a dynamic body of believers, the church and congregations have the responsibility to encourage and promote study, and develop true understanding of the Gospel among all members of the ministry through a systematic study plan linked to contextually relevant mission engagements in respective community. The congregations need to be suitably equipped with skills and capacity to be part of ongoing processes in communities for affecting social change and transformation.

Ecumenical Action for Mission

Wider dimension of Christian faith encompassing the ecumenical agenda to work for common good needs to be pursued vigorously by initiating joint programmes with community based institutions engaged in addressing peoples' issues. Participation in solidarity networks of peoples' organizations working for human rights and democratic rights would enable congregations to appreciate the nature of struggles for survival and dignity. Learning from peoples struggle would further strengthen the mission commitment of the church for justice and peace.

It is hoped that the 40th anniversary celebrations of CNI would result in formulating a strategic plan of action for equipping local congregations with theological basis as well as practical skills and means to undertake relevant mission engagements in respective communities.

Unity for Justice: New Ecumenical Perspectives for the Future

– Richard Fee

Introduction

There is an English expression, "If it isn't broken, then don't fix it?" I am not sure if there is a Hindi equivalent. It is applicable to our discussion of "unity", "justice" and "ecumenical perspectives."

Justice

Justice, by its very definition, means that there is something broken. There is something that has been separated. There is something that has been rent asunder. There is something that needs repairing because the social fabric has been torn. Justice- "justitia" in the Old English from the Latin- means "to join together, to bring together again people who have been separated."

Sadly, this word and its meaning have been distorted by various and sundry groups that claim an offence has been visited upon them and they must be given recompense. They want to fight for justice; they want to demand their rights. The Psalmist declared, "Righteousness and justice are the foundation of your throne; steadfast love and faithfulness go before you." (Psalm 89:14) " Behold, the days are coming, says the Lord, when I will raise up for David a righteous

Branch, and he shall reign as king and deal wisely, and shall execute justice and righteousness in the land."

These plaintive cries we hear both for "unity" and for "justice" all point starkly to one reality-we human beings are dreadfully divided. We all have been separated, we have been torn, and we have been rent asunder. Paul lamented in Romans, "Wretched man and I am! Who will deliver me from this body of death?" (Romans 24:7) We have long thought he cried personally-but, it is this not also the cry of all humanity. A cry for wholeness and healing, a call to be united, a call to no longer be divided one from the other- a cry for true justice?"

Unity
Thankfully the topic I was given to address first uses the word "unity"- "Unity for Justice." This is an integral part of our Christian understanding of how we are to be engaged in the process of bringing about justice in the world.

We should first pause for a moment and ensure that we are speaking about the right definition for the word, "unity". Unity does not mean uniformity! It does not mean that everything is the same. It does not mean that all things have to conform to the same pattern. It does not demand that there be no diversity.

The unity of which I speak is a unity which accommodates diversity. People and institutions and all things human can remain distinct, but they can still be united. The unity of which I speak, demands that a person be able to "see" the other person as well as see oneself- to know oneself. For this to happen there is a primary need for respect. The essence of love is respect.

Paul in his letter to the Corinthians spoke of faith, hope and love, concluding that, "The greatest of these is love." For the greatest value to emerge, it is imperative that a person truly be able to see, to respect the other person. It is when one can really "see" another person, that there can be unity, that a union can be created.

The biblical narrative wherein the blind man cannot see is a story that tells of a person who can see nothing-neither himself nor anyone else. The man cannot see any use or worth in his own self or any other person. When he is made to see, he understands and accepts himself and others so that he is freed to live a life of worth.

The opposite of unity is fascism which demanded utmost uniformity. In fascism there could be no dissention, there could be no discourse, there could be no dialogue, and there could be no diversity. There could only be "uniformity". Fascism believed in force-the elimination of any differences. There was uniformity in Nazi Germany in World War II, but it was an imposed uniformity which could only lead to brokenness.

The Roman military symbol of the "fasces" (which can be seen on many coats of arms of various governments and military forces) shows a number of rods, arrows or sticks bound together, often in the talons of an eagle. Yes, they are bound together. This can, in one way, display unity. But it brings only rigidity, inflexibility and ultimately it will shatter.

The other form of unity, the true unity, is flexibility- a coming together of voluntary association. This is the unity that Paul speaks of in Ephesians. " I therefore, the prisoner in the Lord, beg you to lead a life worthy of the calling to which you have been called, with all humility and gentleness, with patience, bearing with one another in love, making every effort to maintain the unity of the Spirit in the bond of peace."

The biblical story of the lame man who is healed and helped to walk by Jesus speaks of this unity. In his lame state he was immobilized. He feared that he was not like the other people; he thought he was less than normal. When he is helped to walk by the miracle of Jesus, he is drawn forth to accept his differentness. He was not healed to be just like everyone else; but he was healed so that, in his won way, he could walk proudly just as they walked proudly in their state. No longer did he accept the social way, he could walk proudly just as they walked proudly in their state. No longer did he accept the social way, he could walk proudly just as they walked proudly in their state. No longer did he accept the social definition of being lame or handicapped, he was healed to live his life as a life of worth and character. He was united by Jesus with others even though his story was a very different one from the others who walked in their own ways.

Ecumenical Perspectives

The word "ecumenical" in its first popular definition concerns Church unity. The word states that it relates to involves and promotes the unity of different Christian Churches and groups.

The word was called into common use by the Christian family and pertained to the whole Christian Church and the promoting or fostering of Christian unity throughout the world. The ecumenical movement, especially among Protestant groups since the 1800s aimed at achieving universal Christian unity and church union through international inter-denominational organizations that cooperated on matters of mutual concern.

However, there is a second definition which takes the use of the word even further and states that involves " friendship between regions;" it involves and promotes friendly relations between different religions. This wider definition has a more general and universal application meaning interreligious beyond the interdenominational definition.

In both of these definitions it can be seen that ecumenism is coming together not by force to enforce rigidity and uniformity, but rather is a unity that speaks of acceptance, understanding, tolerance, dialogue and sharing. Drawing from the Late Latin form of the word which is from the Greek, "Oikoumenikos" the meaning is "of the inhabited earth". In striving for unity for justice we would be wise to remember what every Jewish child taught to say by heart, "The earth if the Lord's and all that is in it, the world and those who live in it." (Psalm 24:1)

The Challenge of Unity, The Challenge of Justice, The Challenge of Ecumenism in 2010

We are living in a world where three dictums hold sway:

> The globalization of problems,

> The ethinicisation of solutions,

> The individualization of action.

But how do we Christians approach these dilemmas?

Multi-Faith

Jesus was particularly Jewish. He lived in his context of a Jewish family, community and nation surrounded by Samaritans, ruled by Romans; but yet he remained Jewish. The first followers of Christ's way dealt with their own families who were not wholly caught up in the new thinking. They dealt with relatives and friends who were of differing ideas.

We must decide anew how we are going to approach other people-different people- and yet our own people. Like the first Christians-who were converted Jews and reformed Roman deity worshippers and Greek pantheists- we must know how we are going to talk to our relatives and friends. Like those people who heard the message from Jesus and were convinced, we too must learn to relate to brothers and sisters who have not chosen this way. The challenge of seeking justice confronts us in our daily lives. We must recognize that something has been separated, broken, rent asunder and we must come together with those who understand this commission. We continue to embrace our family members, friends, neighbours and continue to walk with them striving to, day by day, mend the broken and bind up the injured.

I would like to share a couple of stories from my experience regarding what I believe is the direction we as people of faith, are headed.

The Dalai Lama

Last year a monk visited Vancouver- 16,000 star-struck mainly teenagers attended his presentation. He spoke from the stage at the city's packed hockey arena. He is 74-year-old and manages to wow the world with his consistent, heartfelt message of the need for universal peace and compassion. On October 24 of this year he will be in Toronto filling our Sky dome which holds 86,000 people.

His message was this: "The future of the century is in your hands (he told the teenagers present). Please take care of it." The Dalai Lama called on the youth of today to do a better job in the 21st Century than his generation did with the last one. "You are the seeds of a better future," he told them. "The 20th century had the most bloodshed ever. More than 200 million human beings were killed through violent action. All were people just like us."

He stated that it was time for a century of peace, a century of compassion. The youthful audience whooped and cheered. Cameras flashed.

"Make the world very safe, very peaceful, very happy. You are the key generation to make that happen. There are still 91 years left. The future of the century is in your hands. Please, take care of it."

The Dalai Lama also advised students not to take their textbooks and teachers at face value. "Read and listen. Then, make your investigation. If you just accept everything, then your brain is wasted." The youth responded. "Awesome, " said one. " He gives off so much energy, and he's funny. He was really inspiring." "He was better than our teachers at school. I expected it to be boring, but he was entertaining. I liked his message that we can change the world by changing ourselves and helping others. We shouldn't just sit around eating junk food all the time."

"He was really amazing", said another. "He seemed very humble, but you could see he was very wise. He was great."

There were Christians at this event. They too were enthralled and captivated. How we receive religious thought is changing. We human beings are being radically altered by the modern age we live in. Christians are not immune.

Eboo Patel

Eboo Patel author of *Acts of Faith: "The story of an American Muslim, the Struggle for the Soul of a Generation"*, and President Obama's adviser on matters of faith won the Grawemeyer Award in Religion from Louisville Presbyterian Theological Seminary, USA. "Religious extremists all over the world are harnessing adolescent angst for their own ends. Patel urges us to take advantage of the short window of time in a young person's life to teach the universal values of cooperation, compassion and mercy." Eboo Patel, a Moslem, is a member of the White House Advisory Council on Faith -Based and Neighbourhood Partnerships and the Religious Advisory Committee of the Council on Foreign Relations. He founded *Interfaith Youth Core*, which is on 75 campuses as a community service group.

Patel says that our challenges are to ensure that we do not conscript God to our understanding of God's creation. We will be challenged by those youth. The limitations of language can become barriers. But we declare that God is the creator of the universe and that God cares for the creation.

Eboo Patel tells of a fundamentalist church near Stanford University which planned a rally which was anti-Semitic and anti-gay. To confront that gathering of hate, another group assembled – 1,000 strong- students from the university. They were motivated by a new group called F.A.I.T.H. (Faiths Acting Together and Hope). Led by a Hindu, Anand Venkatkrishnan, and Ansaf Kareem, a Moslem, this group stood up for what they believe stating"...freedom of our respective traditions to stand in solidarity with others who are attacked on the basis of their identity." They believe they must stand up for any group that would be singled out for hate; "If we're going to have movement of interfaith cooperation in the 21st century, it will be built the old fashioned way- by leaders."

A third story tells of a Palestinian, Sami Awad, who believes that "....his engagement in non-violence should also address the issues that prevent Israelis from being what they should be, to be able to see themselves as humans who have dignity, who should have respect in the international community," Sami Awad shared his experience with a group of evangelical Christians and he told them that when Palestinians can visit places like Aushwitz and Birkenau, the Nazi death camps of Europe, they can better understand where the Israelis are coming from. He said his work is "…about helping Palestinians and Israelis find ways to recognize themselves as equals and to live with the other side as equals."

Global Context

The universal truth that we must all address at the time in history, that will be true for all of our contexts, is that things have changed. Never before could this have been declared so boldly. It is no longer business as usual- for business, for charity, for commerce, for trade, for religion. When Osama bin Laden dialed the emergency response number "9-1-1", the world answered. When the United States of America increases its military budget for one year by 48 billion dollars, it is clear that the world is going to change.

Our Lessons on Unity form our Jewish Roots

In a book entitled, Nothing Sacred: The Truth about Judaism by Douglas Rushkoff (2004), we read, "God is forever getting out of the way so that people can deal more directly with the real business at hand : making the world a better place in which to live." (Pg 33)

Rushkoff explains that there was an evolution of human development throughout the Old Testament. Noah worked to save his own family. This progression implies successively higher forms of compassion, with increasing personal risks, Jews' sense of social justice is supposed to extend past the family and even the worthy, to include all people." (Pg 37) He adds, "They show for Jews, the definition of social justice has an ever-expanding radius." (Pg 38)

He goes on to point out that all Jewish holidays are celebrations of human rights victories. (Pg 38) "The three pillars of the Jewish faith, iconoclasm, abstract monotheism, and social justice, have resulted in people whose very character was defined by a willingness to engage themselves in the plights of others. The Jewish word for charity, "tzedaka", actually means "Justice". (Pg 40)

Rushkoff does not just congratulate his fellow Jews, he does not explain who they are or should be, but he challenges his fellow Jews to re-examine and change. He says it is necessary, "…. to move into this direct experience of sanctity- a personal and vital expression of spirituality- we have to let ourselves grow up. We lose the illusory safety of regression and transference, but we gain the responsibilities and privileges of adults. We lose the magical protection of our talismans and rituals, but we regain their value as affirmation and focal points. We lose the ability to relegate all the hard study to men with long beards, but we gain access to some of the most intriguing myths and thoughtful laws ever written. We lose the authority of our testament as the sole piece of divine evidence, but we gain the experiences of peoples with who we have always been in competition. We lose the special status of being a chosen race, but gain the ability to choose a path voluntarily and to share what we've found with the entire world. We lose the Zionist claim over a patch of sacred soil, but get the claim the entire planet as a kind of Jerusalem. WE lose Yahweh- the one and only actor who is allowed to pay God-but are empowered to enact the unity of Sh'ma ourselves," (Pg 130)

Rushkoff declares that Jews should have a "…willingness to wrestle with sacred beliefs." (Pg 131) " Our iconoclasm and monotheism insure that we never surrender central authority to anyone or anything. Our mandate for social justice guarantees the equal right of each member to thrive. When things are going well, we feel at liberty to experience these truths and exercise "halakkah" as individuals. When we are facing an external threat, we band together – as if we were the components of a single race or organism." (Pg 184)

"Problems arise when one group starts to see its story as the only possible narrative and the characters within it- whether Moses, Jesus, Mohammed, or Buddha- as the exclusive holders of the absolute truth. For eventually, as the world becomes a smaller place, one people's absolute truth will come into contact with another people's absolute truth. When they conflict, so do their true believers. Everyone fights to make the world conform to a particular story.

It is dangerously presumptuous to believe that one's own conception of God is right for everybody. The models we use for God, and stories we have written to explain his relationship to us on this plane, are merely that : models. Divinity, by definition, is beyond human comprehension. To mistake one's model of God for God himself is to mistake the map for the territory. On the other hand, by remaining conscious that our conceptions of God are mere models, we allow for the possibility of pluralism. Whatever, model gets a person to behave as if other people's interests are as important as his own is a good one." Pg 204

" Most of the time, it is not people's religious convictions that set them apart anyway. Our conflicts result from real-world power struggles between despots who manipulate the blind faith of their followers. Driven by their own political or territorial agendas, these leaders use concepts like divine right, manifest destiny, or racial superiority to get their subjects to lay down their lives or justify the killing of others. When people relate to their mythic narratives as historical truths with inevitable conclusions, they presume that the story is a closed book. Their only alternative is to make the world conform to their story, by any means necessary." Pg 205

Fundamentalism- The Threat Against Unity

The recent campaign by a fundamentalist pastor in Florida to burn the Koran drew further divisions not between Christians and Moslems but significantly between Christians and Christians. Many Christians were appalled by this proposed action. It pointed to a rift in the Christian understanding of who we are and what is the great commission saying to us today. What is our understanding of unity? Who are we to be united with? It challenges us on our understanding of justice? From who are we separated? What is it that is broken? How can we work together in unity and with whom and for what purpose? And most strikingly, who are we, when we say we are ecumenical? To whom is God speaking when God addresses "the inhabited world?"

Stephen Parsons in the magazine of the Council of World Mission, "Inside Out" (May, 2001) wrote, "Fundamentalist Christianity is a way of holding on to the truths of the Christian faith that denies any validity to other Christians who hold differing beliefs or understandings. While claiming to be a distinctly orthodox biblical form of Christianity, it proclaims its beliefs in a way that allows no dialogue with other Christians. In short, it is Christianity that does not and cannot listen." Our family of Christian Churches cherishes a tradition of critical thinking and a willingness to be open to further discussion and dialogue. We are all Churches that take the Bible seriously, who respect different opinions, who are anchored to the rock, geared to the times, worshipping an unchanging God in a changing world, using a variety of forms.

Christian Unity In Action–A Global Approach

The New Testament holds up a church which exists primarily for the sake of non- members. No-one can be a Christian alone for long. In the words of Blaise Pascal "....the real strength of Christianity is that it is adapted to all."

Philip Jenkins, professor at Penn State University wrote, *The Next Christendom: The Coming of Global Christianity.* Jenkins argued that the present global trends of Christianity will have an impact on the world similar to major religious movements such as the Reformation. For Jenkins, the twenty-first century will be seen as a time in history when religions replace the importance once occupied by ideology: Christianity will have a major impact on all of the world's belief and ideological systems.

Miriam Adeney of Christianity Today argues, "Of all people, Christians are to love our neighbours. When our neighbourhood expands to include the globe, then we're called to love globally."

In expanding our contacts with communities around the world, It is important to reflect on the power of forgiveness in past strained relationships. As Bishop Tutu once said, "The past, far from disappearing or lying down and being quiet, has an embarrassing and persistent way of returning and haunting us unless it has been dealt with adequately. Unless we look the beast in the eye we find it has an uncanny habit of returning to hold us hostage."

Interfaith Dialogue–Where Real Unity must be Sought, Where True Ecumenism will be Tested

Martin Luther King Jr. stated," Unless we learn to live together as brothers (sisters) we will die together as fools." In building stronger relationships and a deeper level of respect and understanding among other communities and persons of different languages and cultures, one does not need to sacrifice beliefs; instead, we should view it as an opportunity to enrich our faith. People with whom we rub shoulders ought to see in us God's message of kindness and unconditional love for humankind.

Miroslav Volf of Croatia stated in *Exclusion and Embrace*, "There can be no peace among nations without peace among religions. Since religious peace can be established only through religious dialogue, reconciliation between the people depends on the success of the inter-religious dialogue. For reconciliation to take place the inscriptions of hatred must be carefully erased and the threads of violence gently removed."

Conclusion

Our theme challenges us to the roots of our faith. The Psalmist challenged those who heard his songs, (Psalm 133): How very good and pleasant it is when kindred live together in unity! It is like the precious oil on the head, running down upon the beard, on the beard of Aaron, running down over the collar of his robes.[3] It is like the dew of Harmon, which falls on the mountains of Zion. For there the Lord ordained his blessing, life for evermore.

This same theme was picked up by Paul when he wrote in **Ephesians 4** "I therefore, the prisoner in the Lord, beg you to lead a life worthy of the calling to which you have been called, with all humility and gentleness, with patience, bearing with one another in love, making every effort to maintain the unity of the Spirit in the bond of peace. There is one body and one Spirit, just as you were called to the one hope of your calling, one Lord, one faith, one baptism, one God and Father of all, who is above all and through all and in all."

I can think of no greater quotation with which to conclude a paper on unity for justice than a quote from Mahatma Gandhi. His *Seven Deadly Social Sins* speak of the brokenness in human relations, the things that separate and that things that rent asunder true unity in our social interaction. A reminder for all of us of what he said:

Seven Deadly Social Sins–By Gandhi

Politics without conscience

Wealth without work

Commerce with out morality

Pleasure without conscience

Education without character

Science without humanity

Worship without sacrifice

Unity for Justice: New Ecumenical Perspectives for the Future

– Vinita Eusebius

At the very outset I wish to greet all the participants present here today in the name of our Lord, Saviour and Liberator Jesus Christ. I am greatly honored to be invited to this conference and would like to thank the organizers for this privilege given to me to stand here and to speak to this August gathering of Church Leaders, Theologians, Office Bearers and members of different Committees and Commissions of the Church of North India. As we celebrate the historical ecumenical union leading to the birth of CNI we would also revisit the goals of that merger. Our celebration of 40 Years of Missional Journey in CNI incidentally also coincides with Edinburgh 2010, marking a century of Christian mission globally since the historic World Mission Conference which was held from 14-23rd June 1910. Edinburgh 1910 aimed at integrating church and mission, which had been separated thus far. We are assembled here to share and reflect, to ask questions and reveal our experiences on the existing traditional models and methods of doing mission as designed by our churches, so that we learn from and empower each other to be in common mission of God and to do it in Christ's way.

The Context

God's intervention in the human history took place within a specific context (Luke 2:1-2), In my keynote address to the women's conference a day before I had mentioned that,

> "God's intervention in human lives takes place in a particular socio-economic, geo-political, religious, and cultural context. The Church in its entire journey till today was probably never placed in an unrivaled situation of bizarre speed of change in socio-political, technological, climatic and political realities, as it is in our times. The global forces are affecting the quality of life of the human community and the threats they pose for all of life; challenge the church to prayerfully discern the signs of the times to settle on innovations in the mission engagements which would make our presence among our neighbours relevant and "loving".

We need to also consider that the missiology has evolved in our Indian context in response to reflection action process. As we recall the vision and strategise mission beyond these four decades, we need to make sure that this process is driven by the practical realities of mission. Although it is not possible to present a detailed analysis of our social structure in this paper due to limitation of time and topic, yet all of us are aware of the grave injustices dominating our system forming a criminal nexus of domination, oppression and abuses suffocating the lives of many and causing many others to be excluded from sharing the abundance of God's creation and forcing them to live in scarcity and exclusion.

The Mission of the Church is to journey with millions of people suffering economic, gender, racial, environmental, and political oppression, demanding a discernible outcome of Justice and through proclamation, service, advocacy, and care of creation bringing forth transformation, reconciliation, and empowerment for participating in the inauguration of reign of God in Christ.

This paper is an attempt to highlight the causes and effects of injustice and to explore the possibility of the Church being in solidarity with the entire human family and the whole inhabited world to further justice in the world. I have argued that The New Ecumenical understanding of Christian Mission for the future is unity of people in

Christ guided by the Holy Spirit for the salvation of humanity and for extension of God's reign of peace and justice. It is an attempt to urge the church, as we enter into the 5th decade of our existence, to participate more effectively and creatively in God's mission "Missio Dei".

Putting justice at the Heart of Faith

The easiest way to comprehend any justice issue is to look for the areas where injustice is being perpetuated. Some important areas which call for immediate attention of the church are as follows:

Children at Risk: According to Craig Kielburger: *2007, 1-3* With estimates of two billion people living in poverty (800 million in dire need), millions and millions of children lack basic education, health care, and housing. There are still 35,000-40,000 children who die every day. There are at least 130 million children, approximately 20 percent of all the world's children of school age, who have no school to attend.

The World is not fit for millions of children waiting for justice at the margins of our society. Many of them are suffering and dying. To understand their struggles we need to first understand major socio ethical problems in our society today like inequality, injustice poverty, ecological imbalance, migration and wars that put children at risk.

Economic Injustice: Poverty

According to the poverty data of World Bank, more than 35% of the population in India spends less than $ 1 per day and around 80% of the population spends less than $ 2 per day. Poverty means Lack of resources and material. Poor also suffer hunger and the whole concept of poverty is closely related to calorie consumption, physical weakness and malnutrition. Poor live in physical, social and spiritual exclusion and loneliness and they are powerless and therefore vulnerable which keeps pushing them further to the margins. They are traditionally and usually made to stay away from the mainstream and geographical Isolation causes them to stay away from opportunities of education, access to services and information, housing sanitation and even basic things like electricity and safe drinking water is not available to them. They also suffer lack of assets, income, choices and reserves. They are exploited by powers and forced into bondage and exploitation of different types that leads to brokenness and weakness. Their families are big and they have more dependants to support with scanty resources. According to K. C. Abraham, 1982:6

> "Poverty is not merely an economic problem. There is a system that produces and perpetuates it. Broadly defined such system is the one in which the decision making process is in the hands of persons or groups....They not only keep the masses away from the centres of power, they also fail to solve their basic problems of mass poverty, glaring inequalities, growing unemployment and rising prices."

According to Myers: 1996, poor women and men are caught up in a "Poverty Trap" formed of six interconnected and interactive elements namely,

1. Lack of income/ assets

2. Lack of strength

3. Exclusion/ Geographical isolation

4. Lack of reserves/ Choices

5. Lack of influence/ social power

6. Broken relationship with self and community.

All of these elements are interconnected and therefore strengthen each other. A problem in one area means problems in another, resulting in greater and greater poverty.

Diana Pearce (1978: 28) published a paper noting that poverty was becoming "feminized" in the United States. She claimed that about two-thirds of the poor over age 16 were women. Women's economic status had declined from 1950 to the mid-1970s, Pearce claimed, even though more women had entered the labor force in those years yet and women-headed households in particular formed a major percentage of the poor.

Even in India women who are the poorest of the poor are made landless by forces of power. In emergencies and calamities, due to lack of savings they are forced to sell their and assets far below the market prices. Cultural events like marriages and festivals make them poorer, causing them to take loans from local moneylenders who charge exorbitant rates of interest causing them to remain poor and bonded for life. They are forced to yield to bargaining for the price of their labour. Along with all these disadvantages they also suffer spiritual poverty.

Population Growth

India is the planet's 2nd poorest region. Population growth in poverty ridden countries is the major cause of environmental degradation and depletion of natural resources. The high rate of population growth has not only put pressure on the natural resources but has also caused air pollution, contamination of ground and surface water, deforestation, soil erosions, degradation, water logging and many diseases related to these factors. Increasing population of the poor can be ascribed to their exclusion from the opportunities of heath care and preventive health education.

Health

75% of the country's poor live in rural areas and mostly rely on agriculture for their livelihood. According to the Global Hunger Index South Asia has one of the highest child malnutrition rates in the world (Report –Poverty, 2000). Even in the twenty-first century, our country faces ill-health, weakness and different physical, mental, psychological, emotional, spiritual, and social illnesses. States acknowledge occurrence of a few epidemics and infections while some are kept hidden or their occurrence denied for political reasons. HIV/AIDS has reached pandemic proportions in many states in our country. The connection between illness and poverty is striking. It is stated in the WCC document Geneva, 1990:

> "It is an acknowledged fact that the number one cause of disease in the World is poverty, which is ultimately the result of oppression, exploitation and war. Providing immunizations, medicines, and even health education by Standard methods cannot significantly improve illness due to poverty".

Globalisation

Globalisation has had a negative impact on our people especially poor by reaffirming the prevailing ethos of "making profit at any cost". A lot of emphasis has been placed on purchasing which has created a uproar of advertisements in the electronic and print media resulting in the creation of artificial scarcity. People are valued for what they have and not for what they are. Over consumption has caused the devastation of the ecosystem consequentially leading to ecological imbalance. The ecological shift and over production of Green House Gases have resulted in climatic changes. Human economic activities are destroying plant and animal species. Advances are being made at the expense of the over usage and pollution of natural resources and land, air, and water. The emphasis on profit making, competition and private ownership of means of production has reduced the economy of many countries, to one of sheer survival (Ishmael Noko).

Patriarchy and Gender injustice

Gender Ratio is skewed against women. Women and children experience poverty, marginalisation and exclusion more than the men. The fact that Women contribute 66% of the total economic activity in India and yet receive only 10% of the total area's income and own less than one percent of the property makes them the poorest of the poor. Women being poorer than men suffer lack of access over resources and are denied opportunities to make choices and avail opportunities thereby suffering denial of the basic Human Rights related to their survival, development, protection and participation. We need to realize that women are the most exploited and abused of all in the broken world. This truth is even more important today when Global forces are constraining women's lives as never before. Although the world's population continues to grow, the number of women is declining. Poverty is becoming "feminized" Diana Pearce (1978: 28) not only in the United States, but even in India women are the poorest of the poor.

According to the Beijing Platform for Action, 1995

"In the past decade the number of women living in poverty has increased disproportionately to the number of men, particularly in the developing countries. While poverty affects households as a whole, because of the gender division of labor and responsibilities for household welfare, women bear a disproportionate burden, attempting to manage household consumption and production under conditions of increasing scarcity."

The majority of the people living on 1 dollar a day or less are women. In addition, the gap between women and men caught in the cycle of poverty has continued to widen in the past decade, a phenomenon commonly referred to as "the feminization of poverty".

The feminization of growing unemployment is forcing women to seek alternate income options leading to high risk trafficking and prostitution. The sexualization of skills denies women access to government support schemes offered to skilled labourers, farmers etc. Due to Discrimination on the basis of sex many development schemes like credit/ microcredit, land and housing for poor are also not available to the poor women and might adversely affect women headed households and single women.

Education

The literacy rates are low throughout the country. Women and rural population constitute the most illiterate group in the country. School dropout rate here is highest in the world. 46 per cent of world's total illiterate population lives in India and neighbouring South Asian countries and more than 40% of these are women. There are more than 59 million children out of school in India. It is also estimated that 75% of the school drop outs are girls. High illiteracy leads to slower economic growth.

Climate Injustice/ Environmental Degradation

Over populated India also has a major share in the world's environmental degradation. Poverty and population has led to over exploitation (depletion), wastage and pollution of natural resources. Environmental violence has led to soil erosion, droughts, floods and other natural disasters. Dense population leads to pollution. The region is also contributing to global warming due to large scale emission of green house gases. Productive land is being lost due to Soil erosion, flooding, water logging and salinity. Million acres of forests are cut down each year in India, where as reforestation rate is very low. Fresh water resources are being depleted at a rapid rate. Poverty and illiteracy of people in also has led to degradation of the environment as people neither have any viable life sustaining alternatives nor the understanding these resources are not everlasting.

The suffering communities mentioned above, the children, women and poor live in our cities. Sometimes they are picking up rags just outside our churches. They are "Our neighbours" as referred to by Jesus in Luke Chapter 10. They will always have expectations from the God's people and His Church. They are the least of people referred to in Matthew 25. The church can reach out to them in an effort to restore their dignity and rejuvenate our faith which the word says is dead without action.

Mission of God

The important question we need to ask ourselves is "Whose mission and whose world is this anyway?

Mission is the lifeline of the church. Martin Kahler (2006, 1-2) says that,

> "Mission is the *"mother of theology"*. Mission does not begin with the Church or the Church's action in the world, but with an understanding of God and God's action toward the whole oikumene."

God's mission 'Missio Dei' is God's purpose for the world which is establishment of His Kingdom of justice, Shalom and love. Mission preceded the Church and not vice versa. Church is "This worldly" representation of The Kingdom and is also an agent of the coming kingdom. Therefore she has to be dedicated to God in worship and committed to the world in service. Mission has not only equipped the church to evangelize the world but also provided the perspective to respond to the challenges of our society especially in our Indian context with challenging issues like patriarchy, dearth of resources, dalit and tribal issues, cultural and religious diversity. Church can find the purpose of her existence and identity in determining God's purpose for the oikumene. The nature of God as revealed in Christ is love and care of all creation with deliberate inclusion of outsiders. The church's identity and purpose therefore is in being "Xenophilic" / **"Out-Centered".** God in Christ calls us to be involved in HIS MISSION and purpose in the world. We have to first receive from him what we intend to give to the world. Our journey for justice therefore is to move on as one people in our pilgrimage with God and for the people. There is an urgent need to review and evaluate the methods and impact of the traditional mission practices and seriously make advancements to promote holistic mission in the context of Indian plurality, poverty and injustice.

Mission beyond Forty
The overwhelming dimension of poverty in India challenges every individual in the local Christian communities to consider the roles to which God has called us in this world that is troubled with inequality and injustice. It has become unavoidable for us to examine the causes and nature of poverty in our countries and to decide our Christian responsibility in this world suffering from noxious poverty. 80% of world's resources are controlled / owned by 20% privileged people who deny the others of their basic needs of sanitation, medical care and even safe drinking water. Social scientists believe we are in times when we have all the resources, intelligence and technology to end injustice and bring in peace in the world forever. Not false peace where violence is disguised as peace but the real everlasting peace or 'Shalom' where all people share the abundance of God's resources. Why this does not happen is because we do not have the passion or will to do it. Mission of the church essentially is calling God's people to challenge the structures of injustice. The important question is how should we as Christians live in relation to the poor?

As the disciples of Jesus we are called to believe that action for justice and the transformation of life and society is evangelization. The Church will have to recognize that the poor have immense potential to get transformed into eternal springs of living water and therefore like our master we will have to walk a few extra miles and go through "Samaria" to find people who do not matter at all and are therefore made invisible and unreachable by the elite of this world. Each poor is to be seen as seen as someone with self worth having an eternally ratified "Human Right" of "Abundant life". We need to speak out in the name of the voiceless. We must teach them to speak for themselves. We will need the anger of Jesus to set the things right if resources are mismanaged and embezzled. We will have to challenge the forces that cause and support inequality, injustice and division. We have to decide not to accept inequality and poverty as inevitable We need to repent in sincerity for the times we saw hurt and pain and looked away; without doing much that could have been done. We need to show generosity and refuse to take or use more than our daily bread resisting indifference and greed. We need to decide to abstain from the obsession with buying more, spending more, owning more. Jesus said, "I have come that you might have life, and have it abundantly." We will have to commit ourselves to the vision of life in abundance not for ourselves but also for others. God has called us to be generous and also do charity. Jesus calls us to speak out against powers and decisions that rob people of their dignity, health and resources. We need to pray that God will use us to action on behalf of the deprived and oppressed. We need to pray for those who have enough that they may learn generosity and also to challenge those who have enough to resist our world's order of accumulation of wealth. We need to learn to love people and develop a people's perspective. Let us resolve today that we will never be a part in creating an economy that makes a very few rich and leaves the majority without basic resources and without a voice. Like Jesus we will have to focus on the forces that create poverty for anyone on this abundant earth and brand such forces as evil.

According to Hope S. Antone

"Our mission is really God's mission of proclaiming, sharing and living out the good news of fullness of life for all children in the household of God. We also affirm that the household of God is the whole inhabited world (oikoumene) and thus, all peoples, regardless of race, color, creed and faith, are already members of that household, endowed with the image of God within them, no matter whether they acknowledge it or not. Hence, mission has to be holistic—i.e. attending to the needs of the total person; affirming the divine image within them".

The Mission of the Indian Church is to journey with millions of people suffering economic, gender, environmental, political and racial oppression, demanding a discernible outcome of Justice and through proclamation, service, advocacy, and care of creation bring forth transformation, reconciliation, and empowerment for participating in the inauguration of reign of God in Christ.

Unity for Justice: A New Ecumenical Understanding of Christian Mission

Unity for justice means becoming one in complete solidarity with the oppressed. It means that the hopes and aspirations, pains and torment of the afflicted become the hopes, aspirations and pain of the Church. It also means that we as churches be united in Christ and guided by the holy Spirit so as to reach out to them and as a renewed church to be bearer of a message of salvation for all of humanity and also to be in solidarity with those at the margins of the society becoming the voice of the voiceless, the power of the powerless, the friend of the excluded and the defence of the vulnerable. It is not a new idea and according to Justin Thacker, 2009

> 'Integral mission is simply about the church being the church. It's not some new idea – it's the very old one of being what God has always called us to be: the body of Christ – arms, feet, hands and mouth reaching out to those in material and spiritual poverty with the abundance that Christ has to offer.'

The challenge before us is to be an alternative community, resisting the prevailing ethos of making profit at any cost and subscribing to a different lifestyle and value system. Church as an alternative community should be able to project the "one family" image in relationship of love and service to the world. The Church should be known more for her functions and not so much for the structures.

Conclusion

Each one of us should thank God for the opportunity given to us to be a part of this great celebration. As we asses our achievements over the last four decades and identify the challenges lying ahead of us in the present context my prayer is that God will clear our vision to behold the unjust and dominant structures and institutions which commodify and marginalise people. That our minds be sharpened to perceive the oppression of the fringed communities and the exploitation of the biosphere. I sincerely hope that our hearts would be enthused to feel the pathos of those who die each day just because they are too poor to live. May we be empowered to raise our voices in expression of solidarity with the browbeaten and journey with the broken and subjugated.

As we recall our vision and strategise mission beyond these four decades, I wish to quote 2 Timothy 2:15 "Be diligent to present yourself approved unto God". We are called to BE DILIGENT-which speaks of intensity of purpose (building just communities and Just Churches), followed by intensity of effort towards the realization of that purpose.

When Jim Elliot, who was later martyred in the jungles of Ecuador, was a student at Wheaton College, he wrote in his diary, "My grades came through this week, and were, as expected, lower than last semester. However, I make no apologies, and admit I've let them drag a bit for study of the Bible, in which I seek the degree A.U.G., 'approved unto God.'

The challenge before the church is to be a relevant, Just and prophetic so as TO PRESENT- stand before God for a certificate of approval. As a united and uniting Church, which certification are we aspiring for?

Let us set our eyes on this one: A.U.G. – "Approved Unto God" (dokimon parastesai to theo) and with this approval/ certification we can tread forward crossing the threshold to a new decade of meaningful existence.

References

1. Abraham, K.C., 1982 "Mission in the context of endemic poverty and affluence" paper presented in Consultation, Mission and Evangelism Desk, CCA Manila, Phlippines, Dec10-14, 1982.

2. Antone Hope S., "Holistic Mission in the Context of Asian Plurality" double-edition of CTC Bulletin, 2003.

3. Beijing Platform of Action. Fourth World Conference on Women. Beijing, 1995.

4.   Dietrich G., "A New Thing on Earth", ISPCK Delhi, 2001.

5.   Daly Mary, "Beyond God The Father. Toward A Philosophy of Women's Liberation"; Beacon Press, Boston, 1976.

6.   Eusebius V., "Women in Mission: Vision beyond Forty" Church of North India: Celebration of Forty Years of Missional Journey, Key Note Address to the Women's Conference held on 11th October, 2010.

7.   Martin K., "The Original Phrase Is Actually From Theologian Martin Kahler." *Wordpress.com/2006/10/29/the-mother-of-theology-is-mission-conn-bosch-or- franke/feed/ htm*, 2006.

8.   Noko Ishmael "An LWF Contribution to the Understanding and Practice of Mission", Geneva 2 Switzerland.

9.   Pearce, Diana., "The feminization of poverty: Women, work, and welfare." Urban and Social Change Review, 1978.

10.   Thacker Justin, "Church: transform your Community" (3/12/09) TEARFUND, 2009.

11.   UNDP, United Nations Development Programme 1995, 1997, 1998, 2000, Human Development Reports. New Delhi: Oxford University Press.

12.   Kieberger Craig, "Introduction to a Social Justice Issue: "Children at Risk." Vol 3, *http:\RISK\Hill Connections Contemplation -Social Justice Issues (Children at Risk).htm*, 2001.

13.   Kieberger Craig, 2007, "Introduction to a Social Justice Issue: "Children at   Risk." Vol 3, *htpp:\RISK\Hill Connections Contemplation -Social Justice Issues (Children at Risk).htm*.

Serving Justice: Rethinking Diakonia from the Perspectives of the Marginalized

– Daniel Premkumar

1. Acts of Justice as Fruits of Righteousness: Biblical Overtures

Biblical Prophets locate their oracles defending the orphan and the widow in the context of critiquing the cult. For cult has to do with the celebration of Yahweh's saving acts. These acts, in turn spring from Yahweh's inviolable righteousness *(Tzadakah)*. Hence, all cult if it has to be authentic, then it needs to be anchored in righteousness *(Tzadakah).* If not Yahweh shall despise their worship-

> "Your sacrifices are worthless, and incense is disgusting
> I cannot stand the evil you do on your New Moon Festivals...
> Wash your selves clean!
> I am disgusted with your filthy deeds...
> Seek justice *(Mishpat)*
> Rescue the oppressed
> Defend *(Shippatoo)* the orphan
> And plead for the widow" (Isaiah 1. 12, 13, 16 and 17)

Righteousness belongs to God, where as justice is in the realm of humans which they could promote or ignore. Just as the Spirit of God manifests itself through diverse fruits like- *love, joy, peace, patience, kindness, generosity, faithfulness, gentleness and self control* (Galatians 5. 23-24).

a. Overture One: What a Miserable Kick-off for an all time Grand Mission Paradigm

'By faith Abraham received power of procreation, even though he was too old, and Sarah herself was barren, because he considered him faithful who had promised. Therefore, from one person , and this one as good as dead, descendents were born , as many as stars of heaven and as the innumerable grains of sand by the sea shore' (Heb 11.11-12).

- **Isaiah 53**

  Disfigured and abused Servant of Yahweh described in Isaiah 53 becomes source of healing and wellness.

- **I Corinthians 2.22-23** 'For Jews demand signs and Greeks desire wisdom but we proclaim Christ Crucified, a stumbling block to the Jews and foolishnesses to Gentiles '.

b. Overture Two: Jesus asks, "How many loaves have you? "

'When it grew late, his disciples came to him and said-"This is a deserted place and the hour is now very late; send them away so that they may go into the surrounding country and villages and buy something for themselves to eat". But, Jesus ansered them, "you give them something to eat". They said to him, "Are we to go and buy two hundred denarii worth of bread?" And Jesus said to them, "How many loaves have you? Go and see. When they had found out, they said, "Five loaves and two fish" (Mark 6. 35-38).

'Fistful of Rice' is a program initiated by the author in the previous parish where he worked as Pastor in Madanapalle, Chittoor District of AP. The prevalence of HIV and AIDS in Madanapalle was gaining momentum. As more earning men were getting snatched away by AIDS, more hapless widows with many children to fend were becoming noticeable. We at JCM Church, wanted to address this problem. Since the Pastorate Committee holds on to the church's purse zealously, we came up with *'fist full of rice'* program which is easy to implement. All the interested families in the congregation shall save a fist full of rice remembering the abandoned families each time they cook food in their homes. Like in the Book of Deuteronomy- 'In the time to come your children will ask, 'Why did the Lord our God command us to obey these laws?'" (Deut 6.20), children gather around their mothers in the kitchen- 'For whom is this rice set apart?' Once the program became popular across the church, the congregational nurture because of 'fist full of rice' was palpable. Mothers would offer rice so collected in a special drum set apart for the purpose at the entrance of the church. Thus the concerns of the neighbor are brought to the precincts of the altar. On first Sunday of each month, the rice so collected is packed in smaller bags of 15 kilos with the words of Jesus scripted on it- "I was hungry you fed me..." (Mathew 25.35).These smaller bags are placed on the altar and the congregational intercessory prayers for the sick and suffering become concretized in the grains of rice. After the service, the AIDS widows and People Living with HIV and AIDS are welcomed into the church. A helpful talk on do's and dont's is given encouraging the positive persons and widows. After a brief Biblical sharing and prayers, the rice bags are distributed.

On special occasions like Christmas, some member may come forward to offer a delicious meal to the above persons, which is much appreciated by the sick. Now many Hindu and Muslim friends of the church have come forward to join in the 'fist full of rice' program.

Locate Energy for Mission Tucked Away in Parishes.

c. ***Overture Three: Reign of God means Scripting New Lives and Nothing Less (Mark 5:1-20)***
- Good News of Jesus is all about making significant difference in the lives of people. Anything less is not 'Full gospel Ministry'. Why is that most of our church programs remain at cosmetic level? Can our righteousness exceed that of Ramakrishna Mission, Aga Khan Trust and Aishvarya Rai Foundation?

Can We Go the Second Mile?

- Re-thinking Prison Ministry: Prayers and Fruits are Welcome for the Under Trials, But the prisoner's ardent desire is to Go Home

- Constructing New Church Buildings are Fine, but, what About Building People?

PART TWO

1. O Come All Ye Faithful! From Mission Spectators to Mission Partners

Task On Hand: *To enable the rank and file of the faithful to become more effective witnesses to God's reign through acts of compassion and solidarity, especially with those on the margin*

a. *Parable of Oil Tanker*

An oil tanker carries on its back thousands of liters of vehicular fuel. If we further notice, the oil tanker has a separate tank containing a couple of hundred liters of fuel for its own consumption. Strangely enough, I saw in Chennai city an oil tanker stranded on a busy street for lack of fuel. This spectacle struck me a chord about church's own predicament of resource crunch. Except in the case of a handful of local congregations which have evolved ingenious ways of mobilizing hidden resources tucked away among the members of the congregations.

CSI village congregation at Molagvalli Kottala near Guntakal Rail Junction is a case in point. Most of the members are agricultural laborers. Each family has a small tract of dry land. Yet they have pooled resources to care for the poorest among them like- marriage fund for the deserving, scholarship fund for the deserving children, free coffins for deserving etc.

b. *Bible Based Faith Activism: Key to Mission Partnerships*
'Re-reading the Bible through the Eyes of Another'-

CSI Diaconal Services has evolved extensive congregational Bible Study initiatives for promoting care and support ministry among the People

Living with HIV and AIDS. Further, a Bible Study Booklet for the forthcoming Lenten Season (2011) entitled- *Sharing the Pain,* is in process.

c. *Bible Comes Alive in the Hands of Justice Seekers: Story of Ronnie's Bible*

As a Pastor, I began to develop personal touch with the dying in advanced stages of AIDS. Ability to listen to the patients is a rare gift. Listening and responding to the uncomfortable questions raised both by the PLHA and their families is yet another challenge.

Pastors need to realize that there was growing number of infected people within one parish itself. Thus I came across with this young, brilliant, handsome politician called Ronnie, who belonged to my parish. He was infected but did not want anyone to know about it. He thought that the disease will just wither away. Instead, when his health started to fail, it was then, that he was drawn closer to me and so my journey with him and his family began.

As my association with Ronnie was growing more intimate, I had the opportunity to visit a community based care and support project in Guntur District. There I met hundreds of PLHA, of all ages, backgrounds and religious persuasions, but mostly poor. Heart to heart talks with the infected persons and affected families, and exposure to care and support programs elsewhere in the country helped me to delve deeper into the groans and dilemmas of PLHA.

My own grounding and discipline with Biblical Exegesis and Hermeneutics in interpreting Bible from the point of view of the Poor and later in Dalit perspective, has helped me to *Reading the Bible through the Eyes of Other*, the PLHA. It is true that, Bible is the only handy companion the PLHA have till the end. As they grow weaker, the PLHA search the Scriptures for hope and comfort. Many critical questions spring in their minds- about the very existence of physical life; about human worth and dignity as their bodies tend to get decimated. They raise concerns about bonds of human relationships as their own familial ties and long cherished friendships get mutilated. Finally, when they enter the twilight zone of life, they see no glimmer of hope or cure; as the feeling of wretchedness weighs down heavily upon their human spirit –the PLHA seek answers, and seek them desperately as there is little or no pastoral care accessible to them. Hence, *Ronnie's Bible: Addressed to People Living with HIV and AIDS* was evolved with PLHA in mind.. The Bible Society of India has come forward to publish the Ronnie's Bible in 17 Indian languages.

Ronnie symbolically represents millions of PLHA in India and elsewhere. Hence, it is hoped, that Ronnie's Bible would speak to many burdened by the disease, the affected families and loved ones, people of other faiths, health providers, the civil society and the care givers.

PART THREE: VISION BEYOND FORTY (CNI): PEOPLE ON THE MARGIN

Ipso-facto Become the Focus of God's Reign

1. Encountering Contentious Issues? Why not Join-in the Emmaus Walk?

On the day of Resurrection, Cleopas and his companion were walking from Jerusalem to Emmaus and the Risen Lord chose to walk along with them and set their hearts on fire (Luke 24. 13-35). *Padayathra* is deeply rooted in Indian soil. Can there be more electrifying experience than re-enacting the first Emmaus Walk with the Risen Lord in our own localities? As Divisional Chairman, I had 23 village congregations in my jurisdiction. Farthest village parish was 46 kilometers away. Yet we undertook Emmaus Walk to the farthest as well as to the nearest congregation. Youth joined in great numbers and it was not only a spiritual experience, it was great fun. Further dividend was it was also health walk demanding stamina. Emmaus Walk was surely a shot in the arm of the host congregation and their hospitality out-poured. In one or two occasions Emmaus Walk became a powerful statement in solidarity with justice seekers in two villagers facing upper caste violence.

Emmaus Walk costs no money! Anyone could join, young or old, rich or poor. It was introduced by the author in 2005.

d. *Can church boldly address issues which are deep rooted and seemingly invincible?*

- India has richest man on earth while Poverty levels in India is considered below even Sub Sahara African States

- **Caste Stranglehold**

  Caste polarization is becoming more acute with caste politics becoming rampant both in church and society.

- Five hundred thousand villages are becoming redundant the heart throb of India, are no longer able to feed her people

- Do you love your neighbor - the Earth, as yourself? Gen 1 and 2, Revelation 21, 22

  "You make the winds your messengers, fire and flame your ministers" (Psalm 104.4).

Serving Justice:
Rethinking Diakonia from the
Perspectives of the Marginalized

– Shailendra Awale

T hus says the Lord; **Maintain justice, and do what is right**, for soon my salvation will come, and my deliverance be revealed. (Isaiah 56:1)

1. We and Marginalized

We feel a lot of pride and happiness when engaged in the service of society both as a Church and as individuals. Our schools, hospitals and development programs are a good testament to our achievements. In 1970, when the CNI came into being, it formed the Synodical Board of Social Services as an expression of concern for the poor and the desire to show them the love of Christ. After forty years of a united journey there is a need to rethink and redefine the concepts of justice and diaconia from the perspectives of marginalized.

It probably seems quite easy to identify those that are marginalized. Many define them as poor and socially oppressed. But in defining them there is an implicit agreement that these so-called marginalized people exist outside society. A rapid appraisal we has among ourselves, defining the marginalized, none could identify their presence amidst us. Though we recognize that the socially oppressed are submerged within caste and class barriers, we do not identify ourselves with them. They are seen as apart from us creating a situation of inequality. Further it determines our response in serving justice.

I live in Palam Vihar, a suburb of Gurgaon, the millennium city. On a Saturday morning in the last week of September, our domestic help did not turn up, forcing us to manage the household duties ourselves. We decided to go shopping for groceries as there were none at home. When we reached the shop located in community center, we found our maid standing there along with other people from her neighborhood. We were very surprised and asked her what had happened. She told us that the police gave them orders to vacate their homes and return to their native place. Being Bengali speaking Muslim, she was considered an illegal immigrant and therefore a potential security threat. As the Commonwealth Games were coming up, the police wanted to rid the city of its poor as the sight of so many was found to be 'undesirable.'

Our society is ruled and run by such prejudices and biases and focuses only what other people will see, rather than genuinely trying to alleviate the problems of these people. The government prefers that they and their problems be eliminated rather than attempting to deal with them properly. The poor are therefore denied the space to participate in development discourse or share the fruits of their labour.

Against this backdrop we need to rethink who it is that we serve. The difficulties in maintaining a high standard of services with professionalism and the ability to withstand market pressures and generate resources for self sustainability are numerous. But these challenges cannot be an excuse to bypass the purpose and founding values of the Church. A cursory assessment confirms that we are not reaching out to those in need, those who are displaced, denied and dispossessed. Is this justice? Is this right?

2. Contemporary Challenges

More than 77% of our brothers and sisters are living with an income of less than ₹20 per day (Arjun Sengupta's report). The Tendulkar Committee states that 47% Indians live below the poverty line.

Incidentally the poorest districts are also the ones witnessing social unrest. As per the Government of India more than 120 districts are under Maoist influence and witnessing violent struggles to ensure their right to life and livelihood resources. The ongoing neo-liberal economic agenda is privatizing natural resources by corporatising and displacing millions of people and denying them any right to protest against these atrocities. Arundhati Roy has said that there is a serious discontent brewing across the country. Violent means have been adopted by governments and others alike.

The social inequality embedded in the practice of caste and class and the impunity enjoyed by social elites and their friends in power are the real culprit. The marginalized are crying, "Justice is far from us, and righteousness does not reach us. We look for light, but all is darkness; for brightness, but we walk in deep shadows." (Isaiah 59:9)

3. Diakonia

A diaconia was an establishment built near a church building, for the care of the poor and the distribution of charity in medieval Rome or Naples. *Diakonia*, is also a Christian theological term from Greek that encompasses the call to serve the poor and oppressed. The Church is only for Koinoia; generally believed to be the fellowship of believers. Besides fellowship, sharing, participation and contribution are also integral features of Koinoia. Early believers shared common life. Celebrating Eucharist is the beginning of experiencing the gospel. To simply be with the poor and marginalized is not an option for the Church and its believers. The love of Christ must compel us to take forward the mission. *The justice of God has been manifested through faith in Jesus Christ"* (cf. Rom 3: 21-22). How can we redefine the justice in the context of neo-liberal economic agenda and the social inequality, we are witnessing today? No wonder, Roberto Esposito in his book *Communitas* (1998) suggests that 'koinonia' isn't "completely equivalent" to *communitas* nor to *communio* nor to *ekklesia*: "Indeed, one could argue that it is the arduous relation that the 'koinonia' has with the original form of 'munus' that distances it from its strictly ecclesiastical inflection.

4. Justice from the Perspectives of Marginalized

We need to acknowledge that those that are marginalized form an integral part of our community and once we can see them as equal, we can work towards ensuring a justice that emerges from their perspective and takes into account their needs; rather than following a top-down model, where the needs are decided by us and implemented onto them. The recognition that socially oppressed and marginalized people have the ability to make their own decisions about their lives is extremely important. They cannot be seen as helpless people who need our benevolent charity. Rather justice needs to be seen from their perspective.

4.1.   *From Cathedral to Community*

"So now, go. I am sending you to Pharaoh and bring the Israelites out of Egypt." (Exo 3:10)

When Moses saw the strange sight of the burning bush, he thought why is the fire not consuming the bush, his natural response was' go near and see what's happening. 'When we experience the Lord's miracles we too want to be part of this divine act. We want to be close to his presence as per our perceived understanding. We limit the lord to the temples and our role to Sunday worship. However God called Moses not to come any closer to that divine intervention. Then God expressed his anguish, He was concerned about the suffering of his people, their cry had reached him. God responded: "So now, go. I am sending you to Pharaoh and bring the Israelites out of Egypt." Lord wants us to be with his people who are crying for justice. He wants to go and plead to authorities and advocate on their behalf. Where is our spiritual experience driving us? Is it limiting us merely to Sunday worship in a cathedral or does it also call us to be with his people?

4.2.   *From Charity to Rights based Approach*

Rationally, charity gives us the comfort of fulfilling our role and responsibility towards those less fortunate. Compassion is the core to our understanding of Christian life. However charity denies dignity to the person in need. How can we operate in such unequal situation?

If we recognize the person in need is also created in the image of God, then it is our bounden duty to restore him for the purpose of creation and redemption. Ensuring rights is a step to acquiring justice. Transformative justice truly liberates individual. Christ called us to be his friend, as co-workers. Our work of preaching good news to poor cannot restrict to charitable deeds, but it should involve marginalized as equal and important partners and help them in recognizing and realizing their rights.

4.3. *Towards solidarity with poor*

The Church in assuming its responsibility towards marginalized has taken many initiatives. Most of them are like supporting self help groups, imparting skills like tailoring, literacy classes. Such programs do bring economical incremental development, but does not alter the social situation. This approach- 'for the poor' is supported by contributing from our excess. It lacks elements of sacrifice which essentially differentiates the Christian work from the rest. While the Church itself compromised of dalits and tribal, the bahujans, it falters taking position of identity with them. There is need to identify ourselves with toiling masses and reposition ourselves as the Church of the Poor. This new identity would enable us to develop programs leading to transformation. The pathos and pain of these bahujans need to felt and we need to respond with empathy. The Lord said I have indeed seen misery of my people in Egypt, I have heard them crying. (Exo. 3:7) Do we share the same pain and agony? In response of their cry, the Lord says, So I have come down to rescue them. (Exo. 3:8) Their cries are reaching to heavens, so loud and clear, compelling the Lord to come down. How come we are not able to hear? The Poor do not want our money. Marginalized do not seek development project like tailoring classes. Their invitation for us is .. 'come and be our friend'. And those we can empathy with their pain and cry, would be their friend, a partner and coworker in His purpose of creation and redemption. Such *samvedana* would define new paradigm of our work a step towards His kingdom on earth as it is in heaven.

Contributors

1. Revd. Dr. Roger Gaikwad is a renowned theologian, former Principal of the Aizawl Theological College, Aizawl and presently serving as the General Secretary of the National Council of Churches In India (NCCI).

2. Revd. Dn. Philip Peacock is a well known young Dalit Theologian and a Lecturer at the Bishop's College, Kolkata.

3. Prof. Dr. James Massey is Director of the Centre for Dalit/Subaltern Studies and the Community Contextual Communication Centre, New Delhi and a renowned Dalit Theologian.

4. Rt. Revd. S.R. Cutting is serving the Church of North India as the Bishop of the Diocese of Agra.

5. Sadhona Ganguli is the former General Secretary of the National Young Women's Christian Association (YWCA).

6. Revd. Dr. Richard Fee is the General Secretary of the Life and Mission Agency of the Presbyterian Church in Canada.

7. Revd. Dr. Vinita Esebius is an Associate Professor at the Ewing Christian College and a former Chairperson of the Students Christian Movement in India (SCMI).

8. Revd. Dr. Daniel Premkumar is serving as the Director of the Board of Diaconal Mission of the Church of South India and a well known Dalit Activist.

9. Philip Jadhav is a renowned Ecumenical leader and a former General Secretary of the Young Men's Christian Association (YMCA) New Delhi.

10. Dr. Shailendra Awale is serving the Church of North India as the Chief Coordinator of the Synodical Board of Social Services (SBSS).